Beware of a Cursed Forest

Martha Wickham

Published by Martha Wickham, 2023.

Table of Contents

Beware of a Cursed Forest
by Martha Wickham

Chapter One

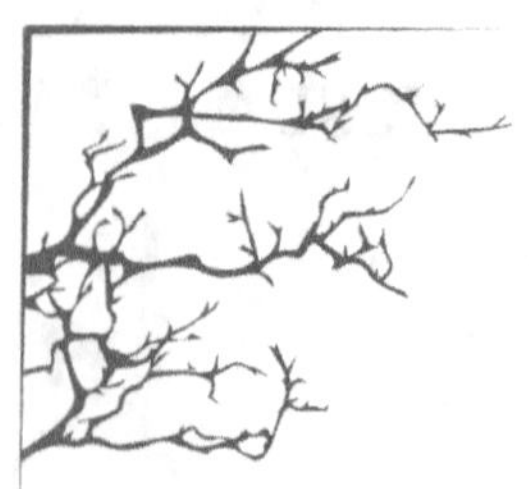

A Small Wedding

"I WISH WE COULD HAVE a big wedding," Violet said watching the evening fireflies come out.

"We don't know many people," Curtis answered as they sat on her grandmother's porch.

"I know, and it would be expensive. I am glad that we are having our wedding at that little white church. The reception will be at the lake. Not ours. I don't want people wondering in our house. One thing I can get is white twinkle lights." She had chosen a white lace gown and a small pink bouquet of roses. Curtis wouldn't see the dress until the wedding. The June sun had finally went down after a long hot day and they had recently graduated from high school. Curtis with a C average and Violet's much higher, but she had no idea what to go to college for. They were all ready for their approaching wedding day.

"Do you want a honeymoon?" she asked her fiancee.

"No, I wish we could just stay here. We'll just spend a few days on the coast not far and come back to stay in my little house. My uncle will be in prison for a long time and he said I can stay there forever. It's mine, I mean ours." Curtis gave her a promising look. "With it's two bedrooms, and his stuff gone, we have both to ourselves. You can work on the yard and I'll get the carpet cleaned."

"Ok, I guess I'm used to it anyways." She opened her eyes wide with hope.

"I'm going to go. I'll see you this weekend at the altar." He kissed her on the forehead. "I got a job as a janitor for our money. That's not bad. I'm only 18."

"Good, I don't want to come running back to my grandma." She breathed a sigh of relief.

"I start at 9 in the morning tomorrow. The kids will get there before I do." There was a spark of light in his eye and she really wanted to marry him.

"I can't wait." Violet winked. "I'm ready so I'll just go pack. After our honeymoon I can come and get the boxes." She went to the front door. "Oh yeah, we're not calling it an official honeymoon." She waved and he nodded, both with love. There were boxes already in her room and she began placing all of her things neatly inside thinking about the coming wedding. Her wedding dress was covered and hung in the back of the closet.

VIOLET TRIED TO PAY attention as the priest spoke the final wedding words. Her husband had just taken his vows and she was tired of holding the bouquet. Finally the last words came. "I now pronounce you husband and wife, you may kiss the bride." Curtis gave her a small kiss and they headed down the isle and out the door. She waited for her grandma as their car waited with their luggage for their 2 night stay on the Canada coast.

Grandma Abigail approached and hugged her. "After the reception, you enjoy your stay at that cute hotel on the beach," she said.

"I most certainly will." Violet's smile told her she was happy to be married. Weren't most brides. She looked like a pretty country bride. "I'll see you at the lake reception grandma." With that the newly wedded couple went to the car to ride to Violet's new home with Curtis and get changed for the reception in an hour.

Violet wore a long flowing semi-casual white dress with a large faux pearl drop necklace, the pearls more than a half an inch thick. Curtis removed his tuxedo and wore a dress shirt and slacks. All of Violet's clothes were in her two large suitcases and the rest in a travel duffel bag. She refreshed her makeup and put her hair up in a clip. They felt hungry, but waited to eat there.

Curtis left talk to his friends. His parents were there, but Violet's weren't. They couldn't afford the trip so they sent a gift and were promised photos and a phone call the next day. Violet missed her parents as she watched Curtis' chat up a storm. Grandma Abigail came in and Violet said, "Come on grandma you're at the table next to mine."

"I don't know if I'll be here the whole time Violet. I'll eat and maybe leave. My arthritis is acting up. I have this." She handed Violet a small wrapped box with silver and gray. Violet opened it.

She lifted the silver antique watch and put it on. "Thanks grandma I love it. It's beautiful." She hugged grandma and loved to feel how soft she was.

"I knew you would like it." They walked to her table and sat down.

"The wedding lunch will be out within the hour, and you can have a salad and roll. Also your choice of fettuccine or club sandwich.

The reception had just started and people were arriving. They only expected thirty. Music began to play and Violet wanted to dance but she didn't yet so she strolled to the lake. Curtis saw her and went to her. "It's a beautiful day."

"I know," she said and hugged him.

"You keep looking at that ring," he noticed.

SHE NODDED, "I JUST got married and it sparkles. Not the same sparkle as the magic ring. Do you think we'll ever run into it again?" She looked a little apprehensive.

"No, not unless it was meant to be and it wasn't. Nothing bad is meant to be. I should have asked the priest to bless out marriage."

"Do we need it?" she asked.

"Through thick and thin."

"That's a yes." She chuckled. "Where's the swans?" With that joke she went to see if the photographer was there. When she saw that he wasn't loud music began to play and couples went to the dance clearing to dance. Violet danced, she danced so violently Curtis stared and her big necklace hit her face. She felt silly but had fun. They began serving lunch and she went to join everyone for the food.

As Curtis sat down next to her she whined, "We got married today. In a few hours it will be evening. We should get a good night's sleep and then head for the coast in the morning. It's a two to three hour drive there. We can spend three to five nights there." Violet stared at his wedding ring, and he noticed her watch. "My grandma just gave me this."

"It's nice. You're right. We'll take a break tonight when the fireflies come out." Curtis agreed.

"I hope that wedding cake doesn't melt. It's the middle of the afternoon."

"It won't. It's the flies that worry me." They giggled and smiled at each other. "I'll ask that we cut and eat it right after lunch."

Everything went as planned and when the fireflies came out it was time to go with grandma having left early. "I'm glad we don't have to clean this up," Violet said as they headed for the car. "That was nice, hot but nice." They got in the car. "I need to get this dress off. It's got two new stains."

VIOLET COULD SEE THE beach from her hotel window. I'm going to call my mom then I'm putting on my bathing suit and laying on the beach." It was their first afternoon there."

"It's going to be hot. I'm going to the hotel cafe for a sandwich and I'll come out and bring you one," Curtis said getting comfortable.

"Oh good. If you can make it a sub," she sounded a little hungry and dialed her mother's number. Her mother was reassured Violet was happy and everything was ok.

"Call me when you get home," her mother said concerned.

"Alright, I am going to lie out on the beach." She sounded excited and ended the phone call. Shortly Violet had her beach bag full of necessities and was ready for the beach. She opened the door. "Oh and hurry with that sandwich. And I want a huge coke with a lot of ice." She giggled kidding. Curtis could only smirk and nod. With things going well maybe they were meant for each other.

Immediately it was hot so she jumped in the water then laid down on her towel. The sun began to beat down so she applied suntan lotion. Curtis approached with her sub and cold large drink just like she had asked. It tasted so good to her. She watched the waves looking for fins but there were no sharks. She intended on collecting shells in her bag. Her sandwich dripped with mayonnaise and vinegar. She laid down and stared at the sky. Far off almost over the horizon she could see many dark storm clouds. She frowned. "You don't think a storm is coming?"

Thunder sounded. "From the looks of those dark clouds, yes. Don't worry it won't hurt us." Curtis watched her eat the rest of her sandwich. Thunder sounded again.

"I knew it was too perfect." She put on a black and white cover up. "When we get home I need to get the rest of my boxes." He needed to give her a ride to her old house. After collecting a sand-dollar, starfish, and a few good sized shells she headed back to the room.

They stayed inside the hotel room and Violet watched the rain pour down. She kept her eye on the ocean as the gray waves tossed and turned.

She left the window frightened and crossed her fingers it would stop. It soon turned to a light rain that lasted off and on until the next afternoon. When it stopped the area was wet and humid. Curtis sat at a small table. "So it's cloudy, wet, and dark. Let's have a romantic seafood dinner tonight. I'll order the food and get some candles."

"Sounds like a good idea." Violet went into the bathroom to get cleaned up and Curtis grabbed his wallet to walk to a nearby store. He found long dark pretty purple candles, matches, and champagne. It would be a honeymoon night to remember. The next day there would be shopping and they could walk on the beach and shop if Violet wanted to. Curtis did have his car.

When he came back Violet was on the couch watching tv with wet hair. "How are you?"

"I'm ok. I called my grandma. She wasn't worried until I told her it rained. Now she can't wait for me to come back the day after tomorrow."

"I've got champagne and candles and if the sun comes out tomorrow I want to walk on the beach and I can take you to a near shopping center to shop. Would you like to?" he asked.

"Yes, I'd like to shop for anything beach related," she said.

"I thought you had everything." He was kidding. He still wore his hair slicked back like he did when Violet met him on the train. "I'll order the food when you are ready to eat."

IN THE DARKENING ROOM the pretty purple candles flickered. She silently scarfed down her lobster and shrimp with sauce and rice. It was quiet because the food was good.

The following day they went for a walk on the beach. The sand was so hot they needed shoes. When Violet began to sweat they decided to go in then go to lunch and a little shopping. Another sandwich would do it and Violet only got a few beach trinkets like a key-chain with shells in a bottle and a large shell. They took selfies by the ocean and decided to call it a day by napping and packing their clothes. Lucky for them the sun had come out just like they wanted and they could leave in the morning and be home before dinner.

VIOLET HAD SEEN HIS house a million times in two years but had never lived there. He had made an effort to clean it up before they got married. Curtis didn't want to get all her boxes until the next day. That was fine. She had her suitcases and duffel bag and he made room in his closet and small dresser. The other room was perfectly empty and his uncle was not coming back. It was at that time just an extra bedroom. She smelled the air to see if she could still smell the cheap aftershave from his uncle Eric. This was her new life. The house wasn't too small so she opened a window to let in some air. She expected to get used to it within a week. She became excited and ran to the backyard. The front and back needed some work. The back was bare and the front only had grass. She would have to ask her husband for money to garden because she didn't have a job but he did. He was being nice and she was glad. The last place to look was the refrigerator. He had filled it with so much food.

Curtis joined her. "There's so much food. Now I have someone to help me eat it."

"What's for dinner?" she asked.

"Anything you want. I go back to work the day after tomorrow and tomorrow we'll get your stuff."

"It's not a palace but I'll like it here." She crashed on the couch. Her new life was beginning and grandma was not far away but mom was in California far away.

VIOLET WAS LOOKING through her boxes when her husband came home early that afternoon from work. "You decided to come home early for me?" she asked smiling.

"No I had to. I was to clean the junior high kids bathroom and they were laughing behind my back and calling me a stupid janitor and who knows what else they were whispering. So I ignored it and went inside the bathroom pulling my mop and cleaning supplies. They followed me laughing, stood outside the door and lit firecrackers. They threw them inside with me and shut the door. They popped and it echoed hurting my ears. There were big sparks and the firecracker that went off in the air hit me in the arm and burned me." He pulled up his sleeve and showed her the red burn. "You know how burns are they hurt forever so I took off for the nurses office to get burn ointment and she snapped at me. She said 'I don't have any burn ointment. Especially not for adults. Get out!' It hurt so bad I ran here immediately for relief." He put his arm under freezing sink water. "I'll call them and tell them where I've went but I'm not going near that side of the school again. Do you understand?" he was just asking because his job was not his favorite place to be. She nodded. "With time I could do so much better than this job. We should both go to school or at least take a class. I'll look into it. As for tomorrow, I have to go back to work."

"I think I will start looking for a job. I am almost done unpacking. Are you ok?" she asked.

"I will be as soon as I put something on this." It was not a serious burn and he went to the bathroom to help it.

As the week rolled on he stayed away from the right side of the school. As things got messy a teacher asked him, "Could you please clean the bathroom today near the fence?"

He responded, "I'm sorry I can't go over there." As the days continued he did not go.

Eventually the principal approached him. "Can you clean the teenagers bathrooms today?" He had heard he wouldn't go over there.

"No I can't. I don't think they like me there." Curtis did not look him in the eye.

"You can clean them when school is out," principle West suggested.

"I don't think so. I have other things to finish at the end of the day."

"You can do it really quick."

"I don't think so. There are other people who can do it," Curtis responded.

"What happened to make you think they don't like you?" West asked.

"They laughed behind my back and when I went to their bathroom to clean it they threw firecrackers at me and shut the door. I burnt my arm and had to go home just to get ointment."

West shook his head. "I'm supposed to believe that. Where would they get those firecrackers from?"

"I don't know?" Curtis shrugged his shoulders.

"If you're not going to do it then go home. I am terminating you."

"Terminating me?"

"Yes, you're fired." The principle was sweating a lot.

Curtis dropped it and went to the door. "The students here are rotten! It's true," he said and walked out the door. Going home he thought about all the ways he could get back at them but would never do them. He had to go home and tell his wife.

"Oh no," she responded. "It will be ok. I have a job interview at a flower shop coming up. You can find another one. Any idea what you want to do?"

"Yes," his eyes lit up. "I'll restart my uncle's gardening business he dropped because he had to go to prison. He had a lot of clients and they must need their yards tended to fast. They also landscape and I can use all his old tools and items he used on the job. I'll let him know. I'm glad I got fired now. I can make a lot of money doing this. I think my uncle Eric will be glad I am. Thanks Vi for your support. This is so much better than cleaning toilets."

"I agree," she said. "I think I'm going to get this job. And it's good we don't have mortgage payments. You will be working on yards and I will be selling flowers. We go together perfectly." She stood there and twisted her dainty wedding ring remembering the old ring she had that chased her up to that Canada life. She twisted it and it let a bright sparkle out. The temptation to make a wish came but being happy she did not think of one at the time. It seemed silly. The ring wasn't magic.

WHEN VIOLET CAME HOME from the interview Curtis' three friends from the wedding were just leaving. Curtis was on the couch a mess with one beer can in his hand and other cans laying around. "I hope you didn't drink all that yourself," she said.

"No," he said and became upset. "My friends and I are planning to go on a trip to Michigan next week. I will be starting my uncle's business afterwards. We will be flying. Is that ok?"

he asked.

"Sure, you can do what you want, just clean after yourself." Violet went in to the kitchen and called out, "I got the job. I will be starting in a few days."

"Oh good. Are you going to celebrate?" Curtis asked.

"If we do it will be with dinner here and I would like to go shopping for new work clothes tomorrow."

"Good idea. I'll cook and we still have wine." He said acting nice to cover up the real reason for the trip. He was glad but he didn't want her to know he was going to rob graves. She wouldn't let him go then. His friends told him they were going and invited him. There were rich people buried in that cemetery and one grave of a young man names Jessie had a legendary ring in it. He wasn't so interested but his friends were and planned to dig it up. They heard Jessie died a horrible death and lost all his blood somehow. He left behind his dog Teacup and girlfriend Tess. When he died she was a mess. They wanted to rob and it would be the only time he'd do it too. He stole when he was a teen but got caught and went to Juvenile Hall. Violet never knew. He got to cooking the best tuna casserole Violet would ever taste.

She came back out dressed in jeans and a sweat shirt. "Things are going great and my grandma's not far away. Soon I'll start saving for a car. Can I drive yours while your on your trip?"

"Sure I'll get you on the insurance."

She sat down. "That smells good. Tuna casserole?" she guessed.

"Yes." He looked at her wondering if she would start making more than him. "It's almost ready." He got the wine. The casserole popped and cooked for five more minutes while Curtis poured the wine. Violet was content.

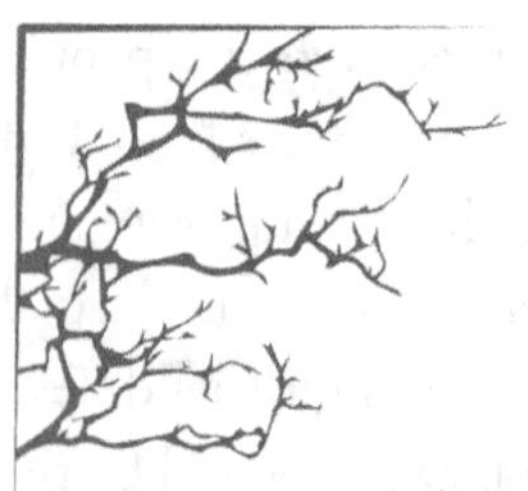

Chapter 2

Obtaining The Ring

CURTIS AND HIS FRIENDS split up into three motel rooms ten minutes away from the cemetery they wanted to rob. They couldn't bring them on the plane so they had to go to a local store and get a shovels for each of them. The plan was to rob Jessie's grave first and look for the famous ring that was fashioned in hell. "I want to see this ring," one of them said. "I hope it doesn't say made in hell or I will run." They snickered at his joke accept for Curtis. All their rooms were right next to each other. After hitting Jessie's grave that night they would look through other graves. The mausoleum afterwards because there was no digging then they'd go for the bigger ones, because they may have had more money to pay for them.

After a quick dinner it was darkening. "Can we go now?" Curtis asked.

"It's supposed to be late but we will all take the rental car and be there in about thirty minutes. It's getting darker at this point. I don't think anyone will see us."

"Have you done this before?" Curtis asked.

"No, I've stolen but not from a grave and this will probably be the only time." By the time everyone was in the car it was darker and they left. They had shovels and gardening tools in the back.

A red glow of light began to come from over the horizon. "I thought the sunset was over," one of them in a black leathery jacket said.

"It was," said the dark blond who appeared to be the leader. He had the most experience stealing and did not spend one day in jail for anything.

As they got out the red seemed to get bigger. After opening the trunk they then got out shovels and began looking for the one grave with the ring. There was a large rounded tombstone straight ahead with some fresh flowers there half dead. The leader went for that one and it read Jessie the name they were looking for. He had died almost ten years ago and there was a card against the stone. It was about how someone missed him so much and how she loved him but never told him enough and it was signed Tess. It was from his girlfriend. The leader left it open and put it back. His friends began to dig but Curtis wondered around looking for graves to start digging. "Go to the mausoleum," the leader told him and Curtis went that way glad Violet had no idea where he was.

As the guys dug Curtis tried opening crypts with the shovel but they didn't come open. When he found an old one with a big crack he decided to try that one. This person had died in the 1920's. He hit it hard a few times with the shovel and the right side fell off. Sliding the coffin out and peeking in he could not see well but there wasn't anything buried with him of value. He put it back and tried to find another one. He kept looking for older graves because if they were buried with anything old it could be valuable.

Curtis stepped out of the crypts and saw that most of the sky had turned red accept a circle of black in the middle. They all stared at it. "What makes the sky like that?" One of them asked. No one responded.

"Guys I don't like this," Curtis said.

"We are almost there," the leader said and he made deep holes with his shovel. "Go look for crypts to steal from." Just then he smacked into the coffin with his shovel. They dug it out and opened it. Curtis came to see. "There he is." Exactly, Here lies Jessie just like the tombstone said.

Curtis glanced up and the whole sky was red. It seemed like an omen to him but there were still pretty twinkling stars shining through. The leader pulled the ring of his finger. Examining it the design looked like hell fire and he check on the inside. It said made in Hades. He wanted to throw it but pawning it would be a better idea. He put the ring in his pocket and they began reburying Jessie.

They kept looking around the graveyard for ghosts and zombies coming to get them for revenge but they didn't. If anything Jessie would have been glad the ring was gone and being the good person that he was wouldn't hurt anyone. They finished covering the grave. "Don't worry. We'll pawn it as fast as we can," he told Curtis.

"If and when we find a pawn shop," one of them said. Curtis was the only one uneasy and they couldn't drive away fast enough. He would never do this again and was sorry he broke the man's crypt marble.

The sky had stayed red for the rest of the night. When morning came it seemed like a dream but they needed to find food and a pawn shop. There was still days left in their stay in Michigan to do with as they wished after finding what they needed.

After Curtis called Violet the leader wanted to tell them his decision. "I easily found a pawn shop in the phone book, but it's not close. So I have decided we have more to steal and we can pawn that before we go back to Canada where we won't get caught. Is that ok?" he asked Curtis.

"That's fine. It's only a ring and I'm not even staying with it," he responded.

"Yes, and it must be worth so much. We can split it just tell your little lady back home your business was doing well." Curtis nodded in agreement. They spent the day looking for places to rob and eating.

While they ate Chinese food in a motel room the leader made his announcement. "We will rob an old mansion. It's old but they look like they have money. Tomorrow me and Anthony will go and see if there's an easy way in and what they leave open or unlocked." All they could do was nod. "Then we'll come back when they're gone and get you Sawyer.

Curtis we need someone to drive the car. You can get out but you need to be ready to drive. Hopefully these people are going on summer vacation. How's that sound?" he asked Curtis.

"Sounds fine. If we go in through the backyard it's harder for people to see what we are doing," he suggested.

"Good idea," the leader Tristan said. He turned on the TV while they had a beer and relaxed. "It's funny how rich people like to come out here thinking that it's nice and peaceful and then get robbed."

Time went by quickly and they went back to their own rooms for sleep. All was silent went Tristan was woke by the sound of hissing. It sounded like a snake and seemed to be coming from the closet. He turned on the light by his bed and opened the closet door. There was no snake, just his suitcase and dirty pants he wore to grave rob. A hissing sound came from his pants. He felt one pocket, nothing. He felt the other one and the ring they stole from Jessie was all he found. A bright gold light emanated from it and he put it in the bathroom drawer to keep it quiet and shut the door. Very strange to him. A little nervous he ran to the window to look out and see if the sky was red, but it wasn't. He went back to bed and the ring could be heard hissing on and off in he bathroom quietly. Tristan smiled to himself, scratched his leg, and went to sleep.

THE FOLLOWING DAY TRISTAN and Anthony watched the mansion they were interested in robbing. The kids went to school and the parents went to work. They went back to the motel and knocked on Curtis' door. "Hurry up. They've all left for the day and we have hours, or at least until lunch, to steal," Tristan said as Curtis threw on his shoes. The others grabbed pillow cases and headed for the car. They headed off to their destination with Curtis driving. They parked a couple houses down and went into the backyard.

They went into the rooms grabbing anything of value or at least looked like it had value while Curtis waited out back. The wife's jewelry, the husband's cash stash, everything they could get into the trunk was taken. It took less than an hour to grab what they could and leave quickly. They went back and left it in the trunk so the motel wouldn't find it cleaning the room. They planned to pawn it the next day anyways. They made off with around $2,000 worth of stuff not including the jewelry. One large necklace the wife had looked like it was worth $10,000. She was into that stuff.

After a cheeseburger they would drive to the pawn shop thirty-five minutes away to immediately get rid of it. They wanted to go home the next day. They got $15,000 when it was pawned to split between all four of them, $3,750 each.

Later after getting back Tristan heard scratching in the closet. Nothing much and he realized in his haste he forgot to pawn the antique ring from hell! It had been placed in the closet because he was afraid of the ring in the bathroom. He wondered if it was haunted. It was definitely cursed. The night before the bathroom light would turn on by itself. There had been a fizzling sound and he knew that knight it would make creepy noises and possibly haunt him for all the stealing he was doing. He needed to throw it out, maybe in the trash. He waited until night and put the ring at the outside of his door. There were a couple small knocks and that was it. He slept soundly.

In the morning he opened the door and nothing was there. He checked the bathroom and closet but it wasn't there either. Anthony and Sawyer, who were sharing a room, came out. "Did you guys see that evil ring?" Tristan asked them.

"No, we did hear some strange scratching sounds last night though," Anthony responded.

Curtis came up to Tristan. "I saw it last night and I took it. Do you want it now?"

"No, you keep it. Hopefully it's worth a fortune. You know they say it grants wishes," Tristan responded and he went into his room to pack his suitcase so they could fly back to western Canada.

"You ready to go?" Tristan asked Curtis.

"Yes, I called my lady and I'm ready." They all pilled in the car and went to board the plane.

The plane ride back was nice. Looking down at the Canadian country side was breathtaking. Curtis sat by the window and didn't say much while the three others chatted and laughed. His friends gave him a ride home and when he went in Violet was standing there. "You're home. Did you like it? What did you do?"

"I'm tired. There wasn't much to do. We just went around, ate, drank beer, and saw the Great Lakes," he responded.

"Well you rest up. I'll make dinner tonight," she offered like she was helping.

"How's your new job?" he asked.

"Wonderful, I'm flowers in training. I won't make much but it's something." She had a calm air about her. She a lot of times looked like that. She didn't know.

"My first job with my uncle's business is in two days. I am going to lay down," he said and she nodded trying to think of what to make for dinner that night.

After a nice pasta salad dinner with strawberry cheesecake for desert Curtis went back to bed. Violet could hear him snoring in the hallway and she went to check on him. As she passed the laundry room she saw all his dirty clothes he had dumped in there. It was a mess and she began checking the pockets and tossing clothing into the washer. In the left pocket of his black pants she found a ring. It was the ring they had stolen. It was big and read made in Hades. She smiled to herself thinking it was a joke. A mockery of her old ring that killed people for her. She put it on her left middle finger and washed his clothes.

While lying on the couch she could hear Curtis' steps so she began pulling at the ring to hide the fact she was wearing it. It wouldn't come off and when he started coming down the hallway she said, "I wish this ring wasn't stuck," and an invisible force pulled it off and it hit the floor two feet in front of her landing right in front of him. "I found it in your pants. It was stuck and I said I wish it wasn't and it flew off my finger. It's magic Curtis! Just like my old ring."

"Give me that ring," he said holding out his hand. "I'll throw it out."

"I want it," she said.

"No, it's bad. Did you see what it said? Made in Hades. There's a bad story behind it Vi. Tristan told me."

"Where did you guys get it? A pawn shop?" she asked.

"No, it doesn't matter. We shouldn't keep it. And where's your wedding ring?" he asked.

"I took it off for a while. Just because I was born on Friday the 13th doesn't mean anything. I'm fine. I will control my destiny." She tried to walk away but Curtis followed her into the kitchen. "It looks like an antique. Why don't you wish for money?" Violet touched the ring. "I wish Curtis had a ton of money." There was a silent moment and nothing happened. She went outside and saw nothing. She went to check the mail and there was nothing in the envelopes that was a check. "Check your bank account because money's coming," she said walking away as her voice faded into the garage.

"When you are asleep I will get the ring," he said not joking. "Were you really born of Friday the 13th?" He called.

"Yes," she called back.

"Have you had a lot of bad luck?" he asked as she entered the room.

"No, just from the ring."

"We have to find a way to change your luck," he said like a hiss.

"The ring. I'll make good wishes." He began shaking his head. "I'll even wish I didn't have the bad luck streak."

"Can it control karma? What do you think?" He was thinking about bad things happening because they stole the ring from a dead man's finger.

"No, it just makes bad things happen if it can. Why?" she asked caring.

"I don't want my time in juvenile hall coming back to me," he lied.

"We'll do this together. But what if we were rich? It would be a wonderful start. If we get one or two million dollars I will let you get rid of it because we won't need anything else," she said and sat on an ottoman.

"Okay," he stared at the floor. "But let me shut it in the closet at night." She nodded. "The hall closet. Deal?" he asked compromising.

"Deal." She held out her hand for him to shake. They were happy and hugged.

In the morning before the day had gotten hot he washed the grease out of his hair. He didn't want to look like a hoodlum any more. He had a wife and needed to look to the future. It made him feel good and he waited for money to come like Violet. Ready to work for his first client it went well. His uncle Eric's business that was now his was starting off good and he wasn't lacking business that first July week. He pocketed all the profits and even learned about gardening and landscaping as he worked. Violet's job was fine as well. She was still a florist in training. It was just weddings and funerals that would be the hardest for her. She completely applied herself. The fourth of July fireworks were like firecrackers going off in his heart and he fell in love with her again. Not a single noise or disturbance from the ring.

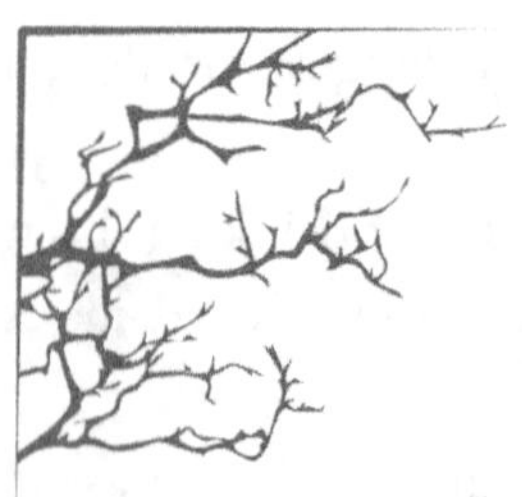

Chapter 3

The Truth

VIOLET STOOD IN FRONT of the door of her flower shop watching the bees buzz by. She opened the door and the hot July sun hit her with it's heat wave. They were only getting a couple customers a day and she was the only one there. She wore the magic ring on her middle finger and made a wish. "I wish this store's business was booming." She watched as more cars began passing by and shortly a customer approached the door that wanted flowers for her dining room. They wandered in one by one until by late afternoon there was a handful of people. It was wonderful and Violet smiled at the ring.

"I am so glad it's picking up," the manager of the shop told her and she went into the back room with a desk. The phone rang and when Melissa answered it she had a big order for a funeral. After the order was taken she got another call. "I think I'll put out an ad for the shop. This isn't even the weekend. It's a Tuesday, slow for a small shop until now."

"Good idea," Violet told her.

Melissa called the newspaper to put an ad in it. "They will be coming Friday," she informed Violet. "Have you taken your lunch yet?"

"Yes, a long time ago."

"Good. When the Canada Times comes they will take pictures and maybe ask questions. What interesting fact could we tell them?" Melissa asked.

"How about business is booming and we will have a summer sale." What Violet was thinking was, *magic ring makes business boom.* She didn't want to say that.

"Right," her manager responded. "I'll be here to help so don't worry and this weekend there will be two employees working." She went back to her desk while Violet sold flowers.

The flower shop smelled good but it was time to go home. Violet was happy with the day feeling tired. Curtis pulled up to pick her up. All she had to say was, "The day went good. Business is picking up." He watched her twisting the ring and noticed she didn't have her wedding ring again.

"Don't use that ring much Violet. And wear your wedding ring tomorrow," he demanded.

"I don't work tomorrow. I have one day off then work through Saturday. The newspaper is coming Friday. They'll take my picture." He pulled onto the road. "I'll wear my ring tomorrow on my day off."

"I know," he said like he was the boss. "Sorry, I just like to see you in it."

"I know," she responded.

"Violet, do you want kids someday?" he asked.

"Sure in my thirties."

When they got home she went in the bedroom and shut the door. "I wish this ring could only do good." There was a flash of light and she knew it worked. This was working but she didn't like the looks of the ring. Hellfire was etched in black. She pulled it off as hard as she could and threw it on the dresser.

As Curtis was lying next to Violet that night he noticed the ring on the dresser. It gave him an eerie feeling and he didn't want to try and sleep so he put it in a drawer in the spare bedroom. He did fall asleep and when he woke he heard Violet's voice whispering to him and calling him.

When he turned over she was sleeping next to him. They must have been coming from the next room.

On Friday Curtis dropped her off at work and they could see all the customers coming in and out. They were lucky they were getting in shipments of flowers more often now. Friday and Saturday would be busier now. She wore only her wedding ring and smiled as she told Curtis goodbye. When The Canada Times came they started taking pictures. One of the outside and one of them together. Two employees and the manager Melissa. "Business is blooming for July. We are getting all sorts of beautiful flowers that are affordable. We can also take payments if you have a wedding coming up," Melissa explained.

"Thank you, that's good to know. I'm sure people will keep flocking to The Season's Flowers," the lady with the camera responded.

When she left half of the customers were done looking and Melissa approached Violet while the other worker Jim watched the customers. "Violet I have wonderful news. You and Jim are getting a raise. Three more dollars an hour!"

Violet jumped up and down. "Oh thank you."

"Thank corporate. They see how the money is flowing in and they hope to open another shop about an hour away. Do you know anyone who needs a job?"

"No, well my husband. Ha ha just kidding. He's got his own business. I feel like this is really going somewhere!" Violet clapped her hands.

"Oh it is. Would you be interested in applying for assistant manager after you've been here six months? You would get another small raise."

"Yes, that's a great idea."

"We can start teaching you about it in the fall," Melissa responded.

"I can't wait to call my mother. Can I use the phone?"

"It's right back there." Melissa pointed.

Violet went excited still unaware that she had the ring to thank. She had made that wish for money. She also called Curtis. "I'm tired of that ring. I heard it whispering to me last night. And I swear I heard it say *I love you, Let's spend more time together,*" he said not confident.

Violet chuckled. "Let's keep it a little longer for luck. It's like a four leaf clover. I was the one who made the wish so the money's coming to me. I think I'll play the lottery."

"Okay and I'm going to try to get a job at the closest tool store. I'll see if I can do that and my business."

"Yes, we'll be doing fine," she responded. "Don't forget to come get me," she said trying not to laugh.

"Of course I won't," he responded and they said their goodbyes. Violet began stocking more flowers in the shop.

As Curtis threw his clothes into the watcher he heard faint whispering again and he couldn't understand it. It sounded a little like his wife Violet and knowing he hadn't picked her up from work yet he ran to the extra bedroom and grabbed the ring. While walking out he tossed it backwards over his shoulder and watched it hit the vent in the floor and go down it. Half relieved and half panicking he tried to see it down there but couldn't and got a flashlight. Shining it down there all he saw was a flash of gold. He needed to pick up Violet and couldn't take off the vent to get it so he walked out the door to get her.

When they got home he said, "I'll call for pizza," while walking down the hall. Glancing into that other bedroom he saw it. The ring was back on the dresser. He went in and sat on the bed. *What made it do that? Was there a ghost connected with it? How do I get rid of it? Will it kill us,* Curtis wondered. He decided going to talk to Tristan and see what he could find out would be a good idea. It had been a couple weeks since he had talked to him but Curtis didn't want to steal anymore. Either way he wanted to talk to him. Maybe Tristan didn't want to steal either.

As Curtis slept a deep uncomfortable sleep he heard loud scratching and woke seconds later. There was scratches on the wall with streaks of blood where he slept. Glancing at his hand he sees blood running down his fingers and small fragments of wall under his nails. They weren't that long either. He was scratching the wall in his sleep and managed to tear his nails enough to make them bleed. There the ring was, on his left ring finger. He noticed Violet was not in bed sleeping and he began pulling at the ring to get it off but it didn't budge. He called, "Violet, Violet," but she did not answer then seconds later ran into the room and saw the wall and him holding his hang. "Did you see this?"

"No," she answered. "I didn't hear anything either. I was in the living room on the couch." They both pulled the ring but it did not come off. It was too small.

"I need to see Tristan and have this ring cut off," he said shaking.

"Is that where you got this?"

"Yes," she said and went to the bathroom to get bath oil. She rubbed it all over his finger and it slid off.

"You're amazing Vi. Thanks," he said and he got up to get away from the wall. "I'll see Tristan tomorrow and see what he says. We have to get rid of this ring." They went to sleep on the couch and didn't notice the sky over them had turned scarlet so dark it was hard to see.

Tristan's house was fifteen minutes away in a nice rural area. Curtis wondered how he had came to stealing. Maybe it had been for extra money. He arrived to the large dark and gloomy house only having been there once before. When he answered the door he was very glad to see Curtis. "Hey there friend. Please come in." They went in and sat on the couch. "Is everything ok? Do you need anything?"

"I need some help with the ring. I had some questions about it. Where did you hear about it?" Curtis asked.

"It's a legend of that ring that has been going around for three decades. Jimmy, this cool dude from the 70's, found the ring. He was very generous and shared the money it gave him with others. Everything was fine until one day he was found with that ring and another ring on his hand dead and all of his blood drained from him. No one knew why and he was buried with the ring from hell. They didn't know how the ring managed to cut all the blood out of his hand. I heard that story from a thief I met in Alberta."

"If that ring killed him will it kill us?"

"I don't know. It could certainly try," Tristan responded.

"I want to get rid of it. How do I destroy it?" Curtis asked.

"You can toss it into the ocean. That might help. You can't burn it. It was made in hell and enjoys the flames. Passing it on is the only option," Tristan said getting comfortable in his leather chair. Just then his phone rang. The caller ID said Anthony. They still did not answer. "Let me help you out. Bring the ring to me and I will pass it on."

"Oh thanks," Curtis said breathing a sigh of relief. "I'll be right back with it my friend."

"Sure, anytime. And when you come back we will have long island drinks," Tristan offered.

"Of course." Curtis waved goodbye and headed back to get the ring.

Tristan's phone suddenly rang again. It was Anthony. "Why didn't you get the phone," he yelled. "I need to talk to you about a robbing job! Now let's talk."

"No I don't want to. I am quitting the stealing life before I ruin myself. I was going to call you back Anthony you know I always do."

"Yes, I just wanted to tell you as soon as I found out. Sawyer will do it with me. Friends?"

"Oh yes and I would like to stop by later and give you an end of stealing together gift. You can even pawn it. A souvenir from when we all went to Michigan. The ring Anthony, and it may be worth thousands."

"Wow, I'll be here waiting," he replied.

"I'll be there soon, goodbye," Tristan said and he threw the phone in frustration because he hated Anthony. He was always so cold to everyone. How could Sawyer stand him?

It didn't take Curtis long to get back with the ring and before long they were sipping drinks and chatting on the back patio. "Are you really done stealing?" Curtis asked.

Tristan nodded, "I'm going to quit. Hopefully I won't start again."

"That's amazing. Who are you giving the ring to?" Curtis asked.

"Anthony, he was mad when he called me again. I've had it with him."

"It looks like the ring is helpful after all," Curtis said and laughed.

"I need to get it to him right away. We don't want to deal with this ring."

"Of course." Curtis understood. The ring sat in Tristan's pocket until Curtis left.

Shortly after he was gone to give it to Anthony. "Tonight Sawyer and me are going to rob this old lady's house."

"Ok, and you can pawn the ring for extra money," Tristan told Anthony as he put the ring on. The summer sun hit the ring and it made a bright reflection. "Thanks for the ring," he said with a phony smile on his face. "I'll see you around." He went inside where Sawyer waited for him.

They were together until late at night when the old lady would be in a much needed deep sleep. While wearing the ring they stole everything that looked like it was of value. Her purse was left alone on the kitchen counter so they wouldn't have to creep into her room and get caught. They shut her bedroom door and took the purse. After getting outside Sawyer sped away quickly.

While riding the finger with Anthony's ring began to ache. He rubbed and twisted and turned but it still did. He pulled but it would not come off. Anthony began screaming and cried help so Sawyer stop and when he did it was on the tracks. They both pulled as hard as they could and it wouldn't budge but his hand bled and it ran down his fingers. The sky was a late night red and the car filled with light. The light was coming from a train. Sawyer tried to step on the gas and moved some before they were both struck head on. They had only moved further in the trains way. They were both instantly killed. The ring, stuck forever, was deathly still as the bright light of cursed magic flew from it and fled to Violet and Curtis's house. It was there in minutes and no one saw it enter Violet's wedding ring. They were both dead and Curtis and Tristan would know in the morning when it was in the front of the Canada Times.

"OH NO TRISTAN!" CURTIS had said this when he read the front newspaper.

"What?" Violet asked.

"Two of my friends that were at the wedding are dead. I'm going to call Tristan and tell him."

"You don't suppose the ring has anything to do with this do you?" Violet asked.

Curtis put down the phone. "I have to tell you something. I got the ring from Tristan so I went to see him and told him I wanted to get rid of it. He asked for it so I gave it to him. I passed it on and he said that would help us. He needed to pass it on quickly and he hated Anthony. Him and Sawyer were thieves. They actually found stolen goods in the car. The police think they were the ones who broke into this little old lady's house. The ring had to have done this. Are you angry?" Curtis asked.

"Yes, but not at you. I'm angry with the two in the accident." She put her hands on her hips.

"I'm tempted to go to the accident scene but I won't. I'll talk to Tristan later." They both went to calm down on the patio before the summer afternoon sun got very hot. While sitting there Violet noticed his finger that got cut up did not look good. The area was a swollen off color and it looked like it hurt. She wanted to ask him about it later.

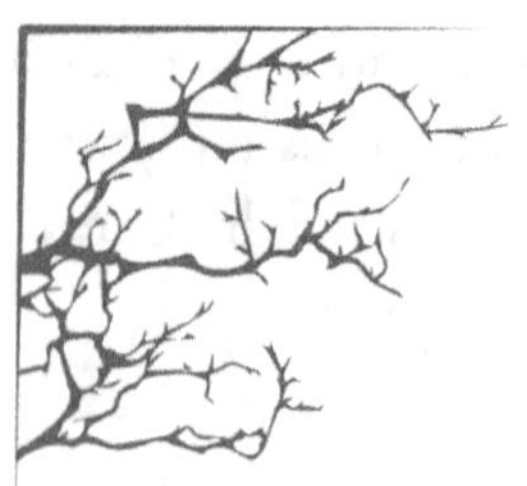

Chapter 4

Cursed Jewelry

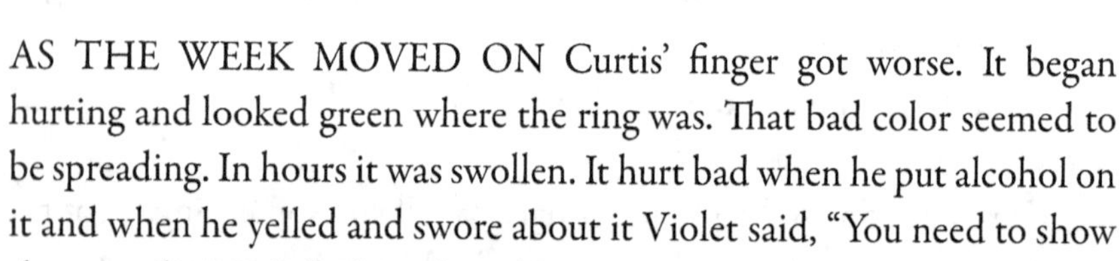

AS THE WEEK MOVED ON Curtis' finger got worse. It began hurting and looked green where the ring was. That bad color seemed to be spreading. In hours it was swollen. It hurt bad when he put alcohol on it and when he yelled and swore about it Violet said, "You need to show that to a doctor. It looks infected." He agreed with his wife and made a doctor's appointment immediately.

Violet was correct. It was an infection and they caught it early. The doctor gave Curtis medicine and asked Curtis where it came from. He could only tell the Dr., "I put on an old ring I found and it got stuck. One night I woke up and there was blood on the wall and on my hands. It seemed like it was coming from my nails. Me and my wife couldn't get it off and the skin just tore."

"Maybe you scratched it in your sleep. Have you had any sleep problems?" the Dr. asked.

"No, more like ring problems," he whispered. "It must have had germs all over it. The ring is gone."

"Good, I also want to do a blood test on you and make sure everything is ok. You wouldn't want an infection to get too out of hand. We'll have her set up an appointment at the front desk and call us if it doesn't get better with the medication. Okay? And make sure you take all of it."

"Of course," Curtis said and he was off. When he got home he took his medication immediately and washed his infected finger. The medicine made him tired and he laid down to take a nap once again swearing he would never steal again. Especially not from someone's grave.

When he woke Violet was sitting in the room. "What did the Dr. say?"

"He said it's infected, I probably did it in my sleep, and to take all my medicine."

"Oh good. It will be ok."

Curtis looked at his finger. Already the swelling started to go down. "Vi I have something to tell you. Those guys that were my friends, were thieves. They wanted me to go with them to Michigan to rob graves. It was Jimmy's grave and my friend told me the ring was legend and he wanted to pawn it. It was cursed and he never did. It was not just that grave. I couldn't find loot in another grave and while we were in the graveyard the sky turned red so we ran and after we go back to the motel Tristan said he would rob a house, pawn the stuff, and we would come back home. That's where the ring came from."

Violet's lip twitched. "Did anyone get hurt?"

"No, and I drove the getaway car when they robbed an old lady at night," he confessed.

"So this is all coming back to you guys. Curtis don't ever do this again," she whined so upset she left the room. Dropping on the couch she didn't know what to think of her Curtis.

He came out to see her. "Don't be upset. Why don't you wear your wedding ring?" he asked.

"It's in the room," she said as she went to go fetch it. When she looked in her jewelry box it wasn't there. She looked everywhere and couldn't find it. "I can't find my ring," she called. They began looking around the house.

"I found it," she called. It was under the couch and she put it on and twisted it. Just then a bright light came from the diamond.

"The magic has exited the rind from hell and entered your wedding ring," he said wide eyed.

"Are you sure?" she asked.

"Yes," he answered and with a mechanical sound the lights started flickering and Violet's porcelain antique doll got up and ran to another room. The ring lit up so bright they could barely look at it. She tore it off her hand and the tv turned on. The sky started turning pick and they ran down the hall. She wanted to blame Curtis. It was his fault. With the sky light scarlet the magic flew from her ring and into her room. The jewelry box opened and the magic light entered the big pearl necklace she had worn to her wedding. For the time they did not touch it and did not look for the doll. "What do we do?" he asked.

"Leave the doll open and hope it runs out the door," she answered and he did. He left the front door open.

Violet laid down on her bed. Not really wanting to she closed her eyes. Suddenly something wrapped around her neck and began strangling her. She couldn't breath. She struggled not wanting to think it was Curtis. Why would he do this? When she looked behind her it was the doll. It pulled so hard the blood rushed to her head. It felt like the porcelain was so strong. Trying to scream for Curtis his name barely came out. It burned and her neck turned red. She reached behind herself and threw the doll far. It flew with the big necklace and Curtis saw! He caught the doll and threw it outside locking the door. He ran to his wife and held her. She was afraid and out of wind. Taking a deep breath she closed her eyes wanting to cry.

Wondering how she was going to sleep that night she said, "I want to stay at my grandma's for a while."

Concealing his anger he said, "Ok, if you need that."

"I do." She wanted a nap and grabbed a cold water and laid on the couch. There were red marks on her neck where she was strangled. She tried so hard to cry but nothing really ran down her face. She didn't say anything but didn't want to be near Curtis. Lying there she dreamed of staying with Grandma Abigail for a while before going and packing.

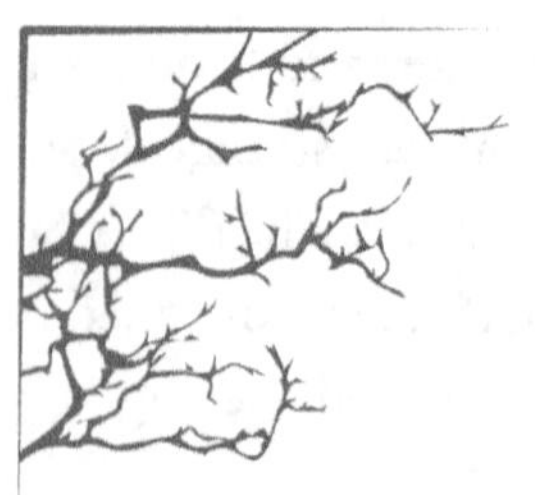

Chapter 5

A Nicer Place

VIOLET CAME THROUGH the door holding her suitcases and bag with grandma Abigail. They weren't that far from Curtis but that didn't matter, she was there to stay for as long as she could. "I'm so glad I'm here. I don't know what's gotten into him," Violet said.

"It's ok. You're here now dear. Just go on up to your room and get settled in," Abigail said.

She took her suitcases upstairs and looked around remembering just arriving there on her birthday. She went to look out the window and saw someone coming. It was her aunt. Violet ran downstairs to let her in. "Aunt Sally's here," she said running for the door.

Violet opened the door and they embraced. "I'm glad you're here." She hadn't seen her aunt Sally Tyler in quite some time.

"You look great. What have you been up to?" she asked.

"I'm eighteen now and I'm working at The Season's Flowers. I got married last June but it's not working out. I'm staying with grandma. I just got here." She turned her head to look at grandma and the dark red line around her neck showed.

Sally took a deep breath. "What is that? Has he done this to you? What's his name?"

"It's Curtis Jacobs, and no he hasn't exactly done this to me it's a long story."

"Let's sit down and you tell me," Sally took her hand and walked her to the chairs.

"I didn't know he was into stealing. He got a job but got fired, now he has his uncle's business to run." Violet didn't look confident because she may not believe such a story. Grandma would. She stood in the kitchen and listened. Violet continued. "Did you know that rings can be magic? Curtis went to grave rob in Michigan with his friends and they stole a cursed ring from hell. I swear. It even said made in Hades. His friend stole it when they were robbing graves then gave it away to Curtis. It started acting funny and Curtis gave it back to the original guy. That was the only way to get it to go. That guy gave it to the other thieves and they died so the curse jumped into my ring then into my necklace. I was just laying there and a doll started strangling me with a necklace I wore to my wedding. I had to leave."

"That's terrible. You have to call the cops and let them know what he's done," aunt Sally said with grandma nodding in the background.

"I suppose you're right," Violet said.

"I'll be here Vi, and you'll just stay with me. Stay forever."

Violet nodded. "Ok."

"I'm here if you need me," Sally said. "I'll give you my number and you can call me anytime. I'm not even an hour away." She wrote down her number and handed it to Violet.

"Thanks," she said. "I'm going to have lunch, take a nap, unpack, and then call the police. It's so good to be back. His neighborhood wasn't very nice. It's nice; we've got grandma's land, the lake, and where's that sweet dog you had?"

"She's in the backyard. Let's all have lunch. I've made mini-subs," Abigail said.

"Great grandma." They ate and sipped cold tea. Afterwords Violet went outback to pet the dog and sit by the lake. When she came in she said, "I need to get a car and bathing suit to go swimming in the lake." Abigail nodded in response.

Violet went in her room and collapsed. Trying to nap it was hard not to think about the police. Muffin barked outside. The thought bothered her and she decided to call the police on her husband to get it over with. She told them what he confessed to her and offered to record a phone call where he further confesses. They told her it would be a good idea because the crime happened in another state and the evidence may be long gone. They said they would call the Michigan police dept to ask what evidence they did have to convict. She was ready to do what it took. Feeling a little apprehensive she wanted to get further away.

When they called her back they said the gang left fingerprints and they could see if they matched Tristan and Curtis' prints. The following day there was already a message that they had arrested him and shortly after they found the fingerprints were a match. Soon came a confession. Curtis had made it sound like it was Tristan's idea and he was just going along. He wanted to because the cursed ring made him angry and he had lost his wife, at least for now. Tristan gave it to him on purpose so he wouldn't have to deal with it.

She ran downstairs. "Curtis and Tristan were arrested. Their fingerprints matched the crime scene."

"Oh good," grandma Abigail responded.

"I want to go back to my house with Curtis and get some of my stuff with boxes. Can I borrow your car?"

"Of course dear," grandma responded.

"I'll go get the rest of my things, then have lunch. I can't believe it's already over. I want to take him back but he'll be in prison a while. I shouldn't."

"You can't. There's no telling what he'd do," she said shaking. She passed Violet the keys on the counter.

"Thank you grandma. It looks like things will work out after all. I should call Sally and tell her." Violet took the keys and left feeling hopeful. Maybe good always wins in the end. It was a nice thought.

When arriving at the house she began loading boxes. It only took three. The last time she saw the doll that strangled her it was in the backyard looking in the window. But where was the necklace? She rolled her eyes as she thought, *the doll must have done something with it.* Violet went into the backyard and there she was, laying by a living room window. She was dirty from the wind and Violet grabbed her. She couldn't find the necklace and needed to. It was cursed, bad luck. And possibly double bad luck because she was born on Friday the 13th. She looked thought the shed, in the garage cabinets and under the bed. No luck. Finally she realized she was in trouble. "Where is the necklace you menace," she said firmly to the doll. Just then a bright summer sparkle of light came from behind the backyard bush. It was a gold tone. Behind the bush the big pearl necklace lay. She dropped the doll and necklace in a box and went to the car to get out of there. On her way back she drove thinking about what to tell her grandma.

"I don't want to tell grandma anything you stupid necklace." She hit the box next to her. There was a loud pop and her car started to drag. She had a flat tire and pulled over to the side. Violet called her grandma then a tow truck.

"The tow truck can take care of the car and I'll give you a ride home. I'm coming," grandma said.

"Thanks grandma. This wouldn't have happened if it wasn't for that stupid necklace."

"What?" Grandma Abigail asked.

"I swore at it and hit the box then I got a flat tire. Remember, it's cursed. I found the necklace and the haunted doll."

"Oh yes. I'll be there in almost thirty minutes Vi," she said and hung up.

When she got there the tow truck was already there and they hauled it straight to the tire place. "Can we drive by the tire place to see if it's almost done? Then I can drive it home."

"Ok, and don't worry about the doll and necklace. I'll get rid of them," grandma said. Violet didn't want to ask any questions and got into the car. The tire wasn't ready so they went home and went to get it later.

"Is that Curtis' car?" Grandma asked.

"Yes, he didn't say I could have it but he is in jail and I needed something to drive. He'll be in there a couple years," Vi said.

"It's a shame."

"Yes and we just got married this summer. I am thinking about filling for a divorce," Violet said. "I'd give you the necklace and doll but it's in the car. As soon as I get them I will. Probably in a few hours.

Abigail nodded in agreement. "Well I'm going to go meet the widows for some tea and cards. I'll be back in one to two hours," grandma explained.

"They are all widows?" Vi asked.

"Yes, all of us. It's a coincidence. With me, that makes five," grandma explained.

"Well have fun."

"Are you going to be ok?"

"Yes, I just want to lie down."

"Alright, and you can have lunch. There's plenty in there," Abigail offered and she was off.

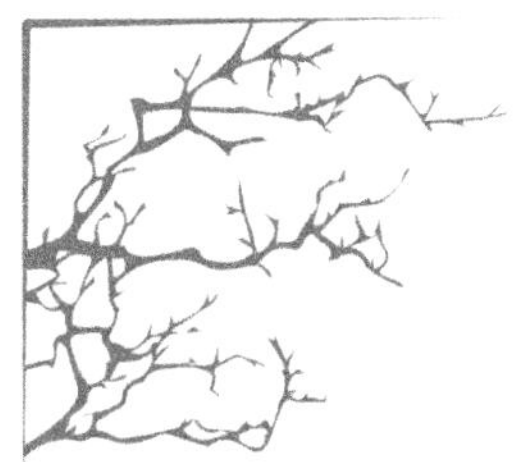

Chapter 6

Bad Dreams By The Sea

By that night they had the car with a good wheel, the doll, and the necklace. Grandma locked the cursed objects in a trunk and put the key in her purse.

"Did you tell your friends what was going on?" Violet asked.

"No, I mostly listened to their gossip," Abigail answered. "I am planning to donate the cursed objects to a second hand store. That was what they had to do though they didn't like it. "I don't like it either," she told her granddaughter, "but we have to. My Violet does not need her life messed with by a necklace and a husband who didn't do the right thing."

"I think he was trying to change. I wonder if prison will make him meaner," Violet said.

"I don't want to find out. I'm taking the items today. I am not going to tell them they're cursed." Abigail grabbed the items and left.

AS ABIGAIL PUT THE items on the counter the man stared at the doll. It was dirty and beat up. He put the necklace in a drawer and said, "I guess we could wash the doll." The dolls arms were bent forward reaching like it wanted to strangle somebody, and maybe that was Violet.

She nodded. The items were goners.

"Thank you," he said and she waved goodbye. Immediately the man took the items to the back and began cleaning them. The dolls hair was brushed and he wanted to put the dress in a washing machine so the doll would go on sale the following day. The necklace he priced at two dollars. The giant pearls weren't real. He put it in a glass cabinet with other fake jewelry. The doll would go home with him. It started to grow on him as hours went by. He had only his wife Judy and daughter Stacey. She was only nine. He couldn't sell an old doll for much and the used items store saw a lot of them come and go. All nicer than this one. At most he might sell it for five dollars.

He dropped the doll in his room and the dress in the washer so he and his wife could fix the doll up. It had belonged to Violet a few years. One of the last dolls she would ever purchase. His wife Judy got a small doll brush from Stacey and brushed it's hair. With a damp wash cloth she got the doll clean. Their big golden retriever was around so she put the doll high up in the closet. Her child had many dolls already and loved them. She was interested in this one and watched the doll that they left in the closet. The dog went into her bedroom and got her small ball in her mouth and ran away with it. It loved to do things like that; get Stacey's toys and steal them. Stacey giggled to herself.

AT THE SHOP A WOMAN with long brown hair in a skirt eyed the jewelry. She chose Violet's old pearl necklace to wear to a business meeting. Her name was Jessica. With a quick small purchase it was hers. It would go perfect with her white suit, and if all went well and she got a raise there would be a vacation in Washington by the sea. She smiled with confidence and put it with what she would wear to the meeting the next day. She sat next to the necklace and said to herself, "I hope everything goes well tomorrow." Feeling better she heard some traffic outside then put the items to wear on her chair and went into the living room.

As Jessica laid on her couch she started to drift off. In her dream she met a very young red headed girl on the beach. She assumed she was in Washington, she had thought about her needed vacation so much recently and hoped to take one. Right after the mornings business meeting she would make the quick reservations so she could go soon. She approached the girl, "Hi."

The girl said nothing but looked at her. She had been staring at the ocean. She began walking closer and got right into Jessica's space. The girl lifted a hand and put it on Jessica's neck, then the other. She ran and the girl began to chase her. She hid behind a large rock near the beach and as she could hear the footsteps in the sand get to her she didn't look up but screamed and woke. She sat up blaming the dream on her worries and nerves. It was unsettling. She got up to turn on the air conditioning and get some cold water.

Early she went to the meeting and tried to pay attention. She was only a secretary and that's why she needed a raise. Without it she couldn't afford her apartment rent and a vacation, but knew she had paid vacation time she could use. At the end of the meeting her boss came to talk to her and as Jessica opened her mouth to speak her manager said, "They okay-ed that extra $2 an hour raise you wanted," smiling.

Breathing a sigh of relief she said,"Oh good. In two weeks I am going on paid vacation then."

"Don't forget to formally request it so we have a record," the boss said as she walked away heels clicking on the floor. When she was gone Jessica jumped in excitement and just wanted to grab a soda and spend the next few hours typing on her typewriter.

When she got to her desk with her coke she emailed her best friend Tory to tell her the good news. *I wish you could come,* she said in the email. *Hey maybe you can. I wouldn't have to go alone. Respond back and let me know if you can. Later I want to tell you about this really nasty nightmare I had yesterday.*

At lunch her friend Tory responded, *Sorry, can't make it. Wish I could but I'm stuck here in boring her babysitting for my sisters brats for a couple nights and working. But me and my boyfriend thought we might catch a movie. Call me as soon as you get to Washington. I want to hear everything. And don't forget to hit on cute guys.*

At least I've got a raise, Jessica said to herself. At lunch she made plane and hotel reservations on her computer. When getting home she slipped into her shorts and t-shirt, turned on a fan, and looked at the large pearl necklace around her neck. She looked good with it on and decided to bring it to Washington with her. She took it off and tossed it onto a chair. There was two weeks to shop, pack, and prepare for a 5-night trip to Washington by the sea. After all, everyone else at work was taking a summer vacation.

She had not been on a plane since she was nineteen, six years ago and was worrying a little. At times she let her fears get the best of her and thought about the plane crashing or it raining while flying on the plane. She always told herself it wasn't realistic. The forecast said there wouldn't be any rain.

As days went by she felt excited and anxious, especially when she went shopping. Jessica bought three big bags of clothing and accessories then made a credit card payment. That night when she finally fell asleep she dreamed it was night and cloudy while she rode on a plane. Thunder was heard as the seat-belt light lit up. Turbulence started then a loud bang. A wing was on fire. It seemed to be out of gas as it plunged for the ground. Jess wished she could hit water for an instant. She looked around the plane at all the people she thought would die. As it hit the ground and smashed she lunged forward, hit the seat in front of her, and woke up. Another dream, that's all but she didn't like it.

It didn't happen that way and the ride was smooth. When it landed she stepped out with her purse and blue bag to a sunny bright day with a slight breeze. All she needed was her bags and to check in to her room. Upon getting into her room the hotel was ok. It wasn't fancy and it wasn't trash. Just an average room to stay in. She wanted to relax with room-service, a drink, and a nap. A tropical drink sounded great. That and a dream-catcher. She was beginning to worry about these dreams and thought about getting, but for now it was rest time. Tomorrow a walk to the beach.

When she woke from a night of not so good dreams, she wasn't so happy but wanted to still walk and lay on the beach. When starting to get her beach bag together she brought her used pearl necklace with her. It was time to go on and stop worrying so there would be no more bad dreams. Bringing a lunch she took her bag and headed to the beach. Finding a nice spot she put down her throw and sat. She wore jean shorts, a white t-shirt, and large straw hat. Violet's old pearl necklace hung around her neck. Looking down at it she decided the large rectangle square links were hideous and she stood up, pulled off the necklace, flung back her arm and launched the necklace as far as she could. The giant pearls propelled it to go far out into the ocean and immediately it was gone. She smirked hoping her bad dreams went with it.

And they did! That night the thunder rolled and there was a storm that shook the blue gray waves but the only thing that woke her that night was the sound of the storm. The rain was actually relaxing and the rest of her vacation was as well. But no worries, the sky was completely clear by the time Jessica rode home on her plane.

IN THE MEANTIME...

Violet screamed in the living room. Grandma ran over to get her. Violet hung up the phone. "That was Curtis. My husband. He said, 'Violet, now I am in jail two years! Why did you tell? Tristan is here also. I am so mad. If I get out of here on bail I will kill you,' and he hung up. I know what to do. I hope the cops were listening in on his phone call."

"We can keep the doors locked and get a security system."

"Good idea, and I don't think he's coming but you should get security."

"I know. I will," grandma said as she went to do so.

August

Stacey sat on her parent's bed brushing Violet's old dolls hair. Her mom came to the door, "Stace, you can keep that doll if you want to. Your father says he doesn't need to sell it. He won't get much."

"Thanks mom." Stacey smiled. The doll was like new. It was cleaned and the white dress was washed. She took the doll into her bedroom and placed it on her white chair. She had her other dolls sitting in a corner. There were twelve of them. A small army looking happy and ready to play. She walked to their golden retriever Sam. "Now you stay away." She pointed her finger at him. He ran to the door and barked. Stacey let him out and when she returned to her room she saw her doll was moved to the corner near by with her other dolls. She looked to see if her parents were around but they weren't. Her mom could be heard in the front yard and she went outside to be with her. Taking her jumped rope from the garage she jumped rope while her mother planted plants.

When Stacey came back inside she went in her room and saw the doll wasn't in the corner any more. The dog was once again in the living room and there on the couch sat the doll. "Dad, why did you let the dog in?" she asked whining. Feeling defeated she took the doll and held it to his face to get it in his mouth. Sam took it and she let him out the back door. The dog ran with it to his doghouse and chewed it a little.

As her mom opened the backyard gate she saw the doll lying in the doghouse slobbery and dirty. She picked it up and shook her head. After going in and wiping it off she called, "Don't give this doll to the dog!"

"He was going to get it anyways," Stacey answered.

"Just don't," her mom said. "You do it again and you're going to be in trouble." Judy was shaking the doll at her daughter. She began swearing about how she has problems with her family and threw the doll onto the kitchen counter. As she began washing dishes the doll stood up, grabbed a small knife and cut her arm with it. "Bill, where did you get this doll?" she called wanting a specific answer. The doll came towards her ready to stab her in the stomach. Judy backed away and the doll lept to the floor! Sam came in hearing the noise and snatched the doll in its mouth. The doll dropped the small knife and the dog took the doll to the living room and shook, chewed, clawed, and growled ripping arms, legs, and finally the head off. With stuffing everywhere it was over. The doll was destroyed. Judy came in and saw the doll parts and screamed. Her husband finally came in from outside sweating. "It cut me," she said bleeding.

He came to help her and they cleaned up the doll and knife throwing them away and also cleaned and bandaged her arm. "Don't yell at Stacey. It's my fault for bringing home the doll," Bill said.

"I know," Judy answered and she sat down to rest from the fiasco.

"I want another doll," Stacey said.

"No, you have a million of them," her father said laughing.

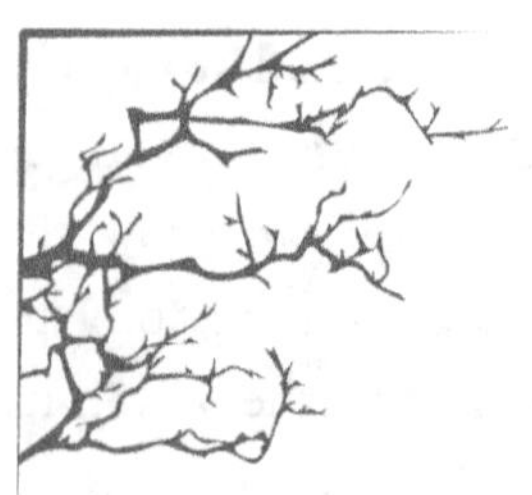

Chapter 7

Misty Falls

THE DAYS HAD GROWN long and quiet for Violet, even when she was working. A lot of the time she thought about Curtis Jacobs wondering if she should give him another chance or move on. When he called her he threatened her so there wasn't much of a chance. It was a saddening thought. He scared her and didn't care. She decided what the best option would be and she needed to tell her grandmother. Entering the kitchen she said, "I'm moving back to Misty Falls. I'll ask my mom if I can stay with her until I get an apartment and they need another employee at The Seasons Flowers there. I'll move my job." Her grandmother opened her mouth to speak. "I will call my mother," Violet said.

"If you think it's necessary. Why don't you just call the police on Curtis?" Abigail asked.

"He's already in jail, so I might just slip them an email. Ruin his chance for parole," Violet answered with a snicker.

"I'm sure your mother will allow you to stay."

"I will miss you. To get a work transfer it will probably take only a couple weeks. I'll only pack my clothes because I'm flying, and as soon as I get off the phone with my mom I'll make plane reservations. Thank you grandma for letting me stay here and all that you've done."

"You're welcome my little Vi. Would you like me to make you a sandwich before I go meet with the widow's group?" she asked.

"That's ok, I think I'll just get a sub." When Violet said that Abigail was out the door.

When she did call her mother she found she could stay with her. She made another call to her place of work to ask for a store transfer. Her manager said that was fine and was interviewing some people that could fill her position. The business was still coming in steady. It was not time to pack and get a plane ticket yet because she didn't know exactly when her new job would start. But found out soon. Everything would work out fine and she couldn't wait to get back to Misty Falls. She emailed her old friend Bernadette telling her she was coming back and would like to hang out. Her friend said she would tell everyone and she was starting college in the fall. It was perfect and with the summer sun out they could go hiking and swimming through the forest. Bernadette's response was:

Alright, that sounds good. You know in the west side of the Misty Falls forest it's haunted? It's considered an actual haunted forest. With me going to school near by maybe we could get an apartment and be roommates. What do you say? We'll explore the haunted forest together.

Bernadette

That sounds great. I'll see how things go. I don't know when my job will start there. I found a ring in the forest before. I wonder what we could find there. But definitely I want to be roommates. Let's explore. Maybe we'll find a treasure. I'll call you soon.

Vi Tyler

I haven't heard anything about a treasure, but I met a girl who said she knew a girl who saw a ghost and a banshee in the forest at night. I would not go out there on Halloween... I will anticipate your call. Just trying to figure out my major now. Later.

B

BERNADETTE WAS VIOLET'S best friend while in high school. She was the best, giving Violet rides to school and her long thick black hair made her seem sweet. Especially when she wore it in a braid. Violet trusted her.

Upon getting back to work the next day and found out she could start working at the California store in three weeks. That was fine and everything would be arranged. While changing the trash she tied it and stood up near the cash register. There was a strange man standing there with a red carnation and huge smile on his face. "Hi," he read her name tag, "Violet. I came here to get some flowers and found the nicest flower in the store." He meant her. He tried to hand her the flower and she didn't take it. "I'm Gary. Nice to meet you." She nodded. He placed the flower on the counter and pushed it to her. "I've been buying flowers here for a year and I've never seen you here before."

"I've only been here a couple months. Can I help you with anything? We have request your own arrangement design."

"No, not at this moment, but that's amazing. You can really tell them how you want it?" he asked.

"Oh yes. We even have books you can look at to find a design and you can tell us what type of flowers you want in it, and colors. When people spend a lot of money on events, we aim to please."

"That's great. My parents anniversary is next month. I'll be back then. Can we plan a date?" he asked.

"Sorry, I'm moving back to Misty Falls, California. Someone else can help you though. Did you mean an actual dating date?" Violet asked.

"Yes, I didn't mean to offend you. Let me fix it. I'll buy two dozen roses." He grabbed two boquets of red roses and purchased them. He pulled two out and gave them two her.

She also picked up the carnation. "Thank you," she said calmly.

"What's it like in Misty Falls? Is there a waterfall?"

"No, I've recently found out that some of the forest is haunted by my old best friend. We are going to be roommates. There's a lot of beautiful forest, and in the spring there are pastel flowers. Do you like flowers?" Vi asked as her manager watched from afar serious.

"I love them. So do my parents. I would love to go to Misty Falls someday. Unfortunately I've only been to California once."

"I have plenty of pictures if you want to see them on my phone?" Violet asked. When she glanced over her manager was frowning and staring. "I don't think I can talk anymore. Can you come back in a couple hours so I can show them to you?"

"Perfect, I'll be back," he said.

"I'll be on my lunch hour and we'll have plenty of time. I can get a sub right there," she pointed to a little sub shop called Little Submarines.

"Alright, I'll be ready." He exited the shop. As Vi watched he seemed attractive. She slid her small diamond ring into her pocket.

The manager approached. "Be careful when you chat Violet. There are customers who might need help. You need to ask them."

"Ok, I'm going. He's coming back for lunch," she walked to the customers to help them.

"That's fine. I'll put your flowers in the back in some water," her manager said feeling better.

Violet talked to the customers but she kept getting exited about going back to Misty Falls. If Gary became her boyfriend and she left, it would mean a long distance relationship. She wanted to meet someone nicer than Curtis.

When he came for lunch they chatted over a sandwich and she showed him the pictures. "Hopefully I'll be in Misty Falls in a month or less."

"I'll try to stop by that town when I am in Northern California," he said.

"Here let me give you my number and email. I'll be staying with my parents when I first get there." She wrote down the info and handed it to him. She liked him a lot and did not care that he was a little over weight.

He wrote down his number. She intended on calling it and talking for a long time. She wanted to go out with him soon before she left. "I'll call you tonight or tomorrow. My plane tickets for Misty Falls are for two weeks from now, so I still have time here. Stop by The Seasons Flowers any time you like."

"Sure, maybe we can get together for some dinner at this great Italian restaurant. Friday at 5?" he asked.

"Yes, I'll be available. Can't wait," she said laughing. "I've got to get back to work. I'll call you."

Gary said his goodbyes then had to leave. Violet had to concentrate on work, but it was hard. This was her last week at that store.

The end of the week came before she knew it and the day of the dinner date came. She was pushing away all bad memories of Curtis and the evil rings.

The dinner was nice at a middle class restaurant. Red candles were lit and she had a big plate of spaghetti. Her phone vibrated and she dismissed it.

"What was that?" Gary asked.

"My friend Bernadette. I can call her later." Feeling glad that over her phone vibrated again with a text. She read it. It said: *We are all headed to the beach. It will be way too hot soon. Glad it's not the haunted forest.*
B.

"Just a text," Violet said.

He didn't look interested anymore. She wanted to get to know him better since she felt like she really didn't know him. "I'm moving back in a week. I'll start packing soon."

"Your house was beautiful. It's a spacious house with plenty of land and a lake," he said.

"Thanks, it's my grandma's. Did you want to meet her?" she asked.

"Sure, anytime." She watched him eat ravioli. "Would you like some?"

She shook her head no. Watching him eat was not fun, but she still wanted to be his girlfriend.

"Now that your leaving, will we have time to get a second date?" he asked trying not to look like a slob using his cloth napkin.

"Yes, any time. I don't leave until a week from tomorrow."

"How about Tuesday?"

She nodded and her phone vibrated again. It was Bernadette. *Vi, I saw the yellow tape on the way to the beach and heard the news. They found a dismembered body in the haunted forest in Misty Falls. It's a male. They found his head. They think it may have been a college student. How's that for urban legend for ya. Call me now please....*

"Can I?" Violet asked pointing to her phone.

He nodded, "Yes."

"Thanks, Bernadette wants me to call her and I'm just going to text her I'm on a date," she clarified.

Bernadette, That is horrible. I can't wait to hear more about it, but I'm on a date. Text me the story if you can from a blog. I have to tell you something about how two years ago and how I got here. Let's stay on this story. I wonder if the forest is cursed. A ghost couldn't chop someone up. He could have been a hiker. Probably just curious. Poor guy. Be careful of sharks and broken glass on the beach. If you stop by the area where he was found, take a picture and send it to me.

She sent the text. He seemed to mind a little, but didn't say anything. Though he seemed to want to leave and she wanted to know more about the story.

Outside the restaurant the weather was nice in the shade. They were quiet during the ride home. When she got home she wondered if he would be calling for that second date.

"How was it?" Grandma asked.

Startled, Violet turned around. "It wasn't that great," she said wearing a brown dress and sheer cover up. She still looked good. "I was just sitting there wondering who I was dating when Bernadette texted me. She gave me the most interesting news. A young man was murdered and found in the haunted part of the forest in Misty. I asked for permission to text her back and he still seemed mad, and when I asked him if he wanted to meet you he didn't seem to care."

"Well that's alright. You're only eighteen. You have so much time to meet someone," Abigail said comforting her granddaughter.

"I feel like ditching his second date. We planned to have one before I got the text. I don't know what I'll do. If he comes to the door without calling Wednesday I won't answer it. Alright?"

"Alright, I won't get it and if he makes me by pounding on the door I'll tell him you're sick."

"Maybe I should just call and cancel it. What a disaster," Violet said taking off her sandals and walking up the stairs to her room. She stopped. You know grandma, I love it here with you and every time something bad happens I don't want to run away, but I'm still going back to Misty Falls. Hopefully I will be back to visit." Grandma nodded.

WEDNESDAY VIOLET STILL hadn't heard from Gary and when evening came he didn't show up. She didn't care, in three days she was going back to Misty Falls. She and Bernadette were going to the haunted forest to investigate. So far the cops had found the body belonged to a college student who they identified as Marty Mason. He was last seen at his dorm saying goodbye to his friends one evening and was never seen again. They still weren't sure if he was murdered in the Misty Falls forest but when they found his body parts spread around the same area there was no blood. When his friends were question they did indeed say that Marty mentioned he was going to stop by the haunted forest to check it out. It seemed there wasn't a college dorm killer, but maybe a psycho hanging around the haunted forest. It was exciting and she wanted to call Curtis and tell him, but didn't know if she should. She probably shouldn't go poking around there either, but still planned to with Bernadette if she could get pepper spray. Bernadette would have some.

She saw Marty Mason's picture when her friend sent it to her. He wasn't bad looking; short dark brown hair, brown eyes, round face. He must have had a girlfriend. What Violet wanted to know was, if the woods were cursed, and did they cause his death?

The time to go came soon and Violet was ready to say goodbye. After hugging grandma Abigail at the airport she said, "I promise I'll call grandma." With a wave she headed down the tunnel to Misty Falls where her parents would be picking her up.

The view from the plane window was beautiful and soon the announcement was made to put on her seat-belt, the plane would be landing. She wanted it to be just as she remembered it. She had only been gone two years. The plane sunk lower in the sky and Vi picked up her purse and bag to go. After hitting the ground and coming to a stop she could see her parents waiting for her outside. They stood in the shade because the end of August heat. School was starting but she and Bernadette weren't getting an apartment quite yet. Truthfully, Violet couldn't wait, and she really wanted to see the crime scene at the haunted forest.

Exiting the plane she happily greeted her parents with hugs. Her mom looked ecstatic to see her again. "Violet, we will get your bags then lunch!" Vi gladly agreed. The rest of her first day back consisted of resting mostly. She stood in her room feeling sentimental. She had left it a mess, but her parents had cleaned it up for her. Her father came in and dropped off her two suitcases. Her stuffed rabbit was still there and her white ruffled curtains too. She lay on her bed staring at the long full length mirror, and her parents had given her a fan for the hot weather. Before taking a nap, she decided to call Bernadette. They were so happy to talk and made plans to visit the haunted forest and check out the crime scene. "Any news on the murder?"

"No they have no idea who did it," Bernadette responded. "But the body parts were all around. They are burying them this weekend without a viewing. Want to go? I can find where it's at."

"I don't want to impose, so no. I just want to go to the haunted forest tomorrow and take pictures, just please not at night Bernadette," Violet pleaded.

"Ok," she said. "You may actually take a picture of a ghost on accident. That has been known to happen. We'll go right before lunch so if you find a finger, you won't throw up," Bernadette laughed.

"Bernie, that was funny, but there is a murderer on the loose. The cops must be worried and watching," Violet said.

"Yeah."

"I'll see you tomorrow."

"And I want to look for an apartment this week. One near the dorm."

"Where the murdered kid was staying?" Violet asked.

"Yes, well I've started school and the dorm is right near the school. I have to go and I am going to be a student worker to help pay the rent." Bernadette was serious.

"I've gotta go. My mom's made a huge dinner with my dad for my return. Backyard barbecue with beans, salad, french fries, potato salad, and cheeseburgers."

"Ok, where's the barbecue?"

"I don't know. I guess it's just a backyard grill," Violet said. They giggled and hung up.

At the dinner they ate on the patio while the sun lowered in the sky. Violet dipped her chips in her potato salad. "What are you thinking about?" Her mother asked her.

"Tomorrow me and Bernadette are going to the haunted forest to look around. That's not where I found the rind."

"That's fine. Do you have anything else planned?" Her mom asked.

"Just lunch, and later this week we are going to look for an apartment near the school. We want to live together as roommates."

Her mom put down her cheeseburger. "You girls just be careful. A boy that went to that school was murdered."

"I know, Bernie told me. I've been wanting to go to the haunted forest since she told me. I heard it's beautiful, but creepy." Violet dug into her large hamburger.

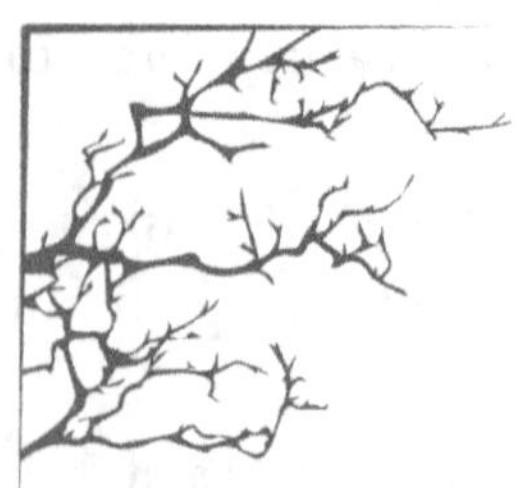

Chapter 8

Mystery Forest

Violet woke up that morning ready to face the day. The news told her the police questioned Marty Mason's parents and found they hadn't even spoken to him. It seemed to be just a random killing, which made the area much more dangerous. She got on her boots and prepare to meet the forest. She put necessities and snacks in her backpack and when the doorbell rang she was ready for Bernadette. "Hi Mrs. Tyler," her friend said.

"Hey there Bernadette." Bonnie Tyler did not remember this friend of her daughters, but knew her name because her daughter told her. "You guys be careful. If you want you can take sodas," Bonnie said glad her only child was home. They did grab one and were off. The haunted forest was 40 minutes away.

When they began passing forest Bernadette said, "We're almost to the haunted part. They pulled over in a parking spot that was dirt that looked like curious people parked there before. "That is where they found the body parts, I think." she pointed.

Violet began taking pictures with her phone. She looked around for objects.

"What are you looking for?" Bernadette asked.

"Clues, anything," Violet said staring at the ground.

"We'll keep looking." The bushes rustled hard. They went to see it, but nothing was there. Not even a breeze. It happened two more times and they thought it could be an animal. "The police covered the area pretty good."

"Did they bring dogs?" Violet asked.

"No."

"Then we'll keep looking." Violet got on the trail and waited for Bernadette to follow her. They began walking watching the area. Finally something sparkled in the sun. They ran over. It was a gold key! Violet picked it up. "It may have belonged to the dead kid." She took a few pictures of the area with her camera.

"Do you want to come back when night falls?" Bernadette asked.

"No, what for? I don't want to see ghosts. Do you?"

"Not ever."

"Let's look around off the path." In agreement they left the path and walked towards a small hill. There was nothing but a few wrappers that someone threw. In that area there was no flowers, just grass and really tall trees, some birds and a woodpecker was heard pecking. "I hope that's a woodpecker," Violet said shakily and her friend agreed. A small breeze began blowing in their direction and the bushes were fanned their way. Pushed hard by a heavy wind that seemed directed towards them. As if something was coming a cracking sound could be heard echoing in the distance. As it continued the girls looked at each other, and quickly ran as fast as their feet could carry them to the car. After locking the doors the wind began shaking a car.

"It's like we woke a ghost," Bernadette said starting the car. Driving down the street, Violet could see the haunted forest blowing violently in wind but was the place disturbed by wind.

"We're dead now," Violet said. "We shouldn't have taken the key."

"Keep it. We need to give it to the police." They drove away feeling temporarily safe.

Violet took one last picture behind them. "I don't think I could eat now."

"Let's go to my house." When Bernadette got home she made them both sandwiches. Violet ate a little.

"I think that key I found belongs to the dead guy," Violet said chewing her sandwich.

"Yes, I bet you I could figure out which room he was in if I go to the dorm. We won't have many aprtment complexes to look at. I think I want to be in the closest apartment to the school, and that's only one complex. It's not in bad shape. Let's go look in a little while."

"How can you be so calm? The wind from a haunted forest tried to kill us!" Violet said just letting her know.

"It was only wind, wind that was destined to tell us a murdered person was there. So, what do you think?" Bernadette asked.

"It's fine. I think we're fine for now. I start work this week and I'll be training for assistant manager. I'm going to get myself a car. A real cheapo I can drive for now."

"I'll be working at the school as a teacher's assistant. Do you think that murdered kid had a roommate?"

"No, but I'm not sure."

"I'll find out where his room was and we'll go try the key." Bernadette sounded confident. After eating, they put a down payment on an apartment; two bedrooms, one bath and a spacious living room, it was perfect. It had white blinds and brown carpet that was perfectly clean. They couldn't wait to move in.

"I may need to go furniture shopping, for affordable stuff," Violet said.

"We both do, and we definitely need plants. It will make it seem more comfortable until we get used to it. The good thing is the door has a chain to keep us safer from the murderer. We will always keep it locked." Violet agreed. They both held a key.

"I can't wait to move in," Violet said. "I'll start packing when I get home."

"I'm going to move in as soon as I can too," Bernadette said.

When Violet got home she ran to her room to rest. Her mom asked, "Are you going to take a nap?"

"I'll just lay here and rest. Do we have empty boxes in the garage? Me and Bernadette found an apartment."

Her mother nodded.

"I want you to stop by and see it. I saved a little money staying at grandma's. I want to get an affordable car before I move out. Remember they have promoted me to assistant manager at The Season's Flowers. Bernadette will probably move in before me."

"You're father saw a car parked that had a for sale sign on it. It's a small light blue car, about fifteen years old but looks good. He'll call and you both can take it for a test drive tomorrow, ok?"

"That's fine mom. Sounds nice." Violet hopped up to collect boxes to pack. After finishing some packing and eating dinner she fell asleep and didn't wake until nightfall. While laying on her bed she picked up the key she found. It looked new. The sound of small things moving in the kitchen could be heard. The house was silent. When she got up she headed into the kitchen and saw some small appliances were moved and the refrigerator had been pulled out far. It was either her parents or a ghost. But why would Mary's ghost haunt her when they wanted his murderer to get caught? Maybe it was because she had the key. Maybe it wasn't him but another ghost that had followed them home from the haunted forest.

Why was the wind chasing them? She wanted to see if people had similar experiences to theirs so she did an internet search. Sure enough they had. No one could explain the strange happenings and ghost sittings in the forest. The only assumption was some of the ghosts had been murdered and dumped there. At the bottom of the search results came striking news. Two more bodies had been found in the haunted forest. This time they weren't dismembered. They were a young man and woman, and unfortunately went to Bernadette's school. The blog did say that if the college campus murders continued they would shut the school down. It was probably only a threat, and they wanted to hire campus and dorm security. That would be a good idea, but it didn't seem like such a good choice to live near there. And Bernadette needed to go to school. Her job was there. She would be moving into their new apartment in the next couple of days.

"Who moved the refrigerator?" her mom called from the kitchen.

"I don't know. I heard it move."

"Violet, this had better not be a prank," her mom said.

"I don't know, but I'm sleeping with my door locked tonight. And the college campus murderer has struck again."

"Maybe you shouldn't move into that apartment yet," her mom suggested.

"You're right. I think I will hold off until they catch him. I have a feeling they will catch him soon. And the school might hire security." Her mom nodded her approval. The boxes of stuffed animals, books, etc would stay in her room a little longer. Violet did get that car her father wanted her to see and it wasn't that bad. It wasn't perfect, but it ran. She didn't mind spending the money because she didn't think she was moving quite yet.

That first night with her car she heard sounds again. It sounded like small items dropping in the kitchen. She ignored it, maybe it was mice. Maybe she should get a cat. A cat would be perfect. She got out of bed and went into her mothers room. "Mom, what ever happened to Inky? My boo boo."

"When you left we gave her to your aunt Theresa. I just said she could keep her for a while. She has lots of pets. Maybe you could get her back now. Do you want to?" Her mother Bonnie responded in bed.

"I would love that," Violet said excitedly. "I miss ol' Inky. He was my best friend. Remember when I found that ring? It was only two years ago, I made a wish and there was Inky. All black with his white spot in front of him. I don't know if the universe made him for me, or if he was just some stray who wanted to be rescued. I wonder how old he is. Thanks mom," she said with a smile and went back to bed and closed her eyes. One of her boxes moved three inches. She sat up when she heard that.

What did that? Was it residual, past events repeating themselves because of the key, or was it a conscious ghost? Probably a ghost. The only way to know would be to ask a psychic or try to communicate with it with Bernadette. They could try later, for now there was a murder to solve and the cops had no clue who it was.

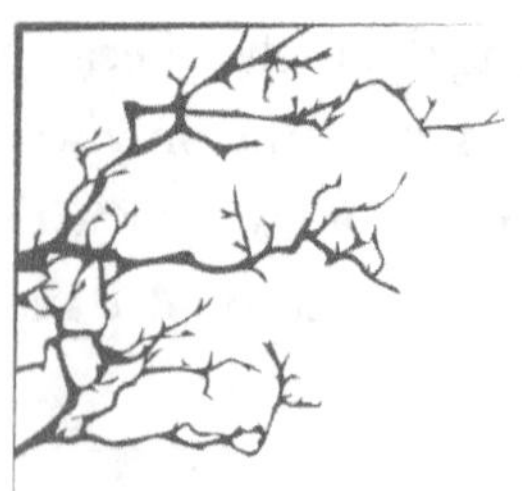

Chapter 9

The Rescues

The day of Marty's death

"I'm thinking about heading to the haunted forest. Want to come?" Marty Mason asked.

"That's ok. I've got studying to do," his friend Tim responded holding a small armful of books.

"My girlfriend and I have a dinner date." Rob's brunette girlfriend hung on to his arm and batted her lashes. The sun was lower in the sky that end of August day. School had just started and had been exited about it and the new dorm they were staying in. It stood tall like an apartment complex.

"Alright, I had heard some ghost stories about fairies and ghosts peaking around corners. Some of it is residual. The ghosts aren't even conscious. I don't know how, maybe they're just images of people that were there a long time ago. They should call it the faerie forest. I'm going. I'll let you know what happens," Marty said as he headed off into his car quickly. It was the one last thing he wanted to do before summer ended, he would just have to do it alone. It was evening and there was two more hours until it got dark and he could see a ghost.

He spent some time having dinner in a fast food restaurant. After burning that time he headed for the forty-five minute drive. When he got there he would just walk around or sit somewhere like his car. He finally found a dirt space by the road to park. It was large and beautiful. Maybe they should have actually changed the name to the emerald forest. Not dark yet he decided to walk around and explore before the ghosts got there.

There were plenty of sounds; leaves rustling, squirrels tossing nuts, and wind. Walking down a path he stopped. There was still the sound of footsteps. He shook his head and walked further down and just kept walking until her got to a small pond. Sitting down on a large rock he waited until it was dark, minutes away. A little afraid of ghosts he wanted to stick to the path so he could find his car easy if a ghost chased him. Night soon fell and crickets chirped. There were again footsteps. He looked around. There was all kinds of sounds that way. A ghost. He walked towards that way hoping for a sight of it. Something was coming and he hid behind a large leafy bush. A figure in black went to where he was. It was a person. They had a black cloth mask and were dressed all in black. They knew he had been there. On the man's side was a knife and on it was blood! Marty turned and ran for his car as fast as his legs could take him down the path. Soon the dark man was behind him and he threw his knife at Marty. Injuring his leg he fell to the ground. The man stabbed him again so he could drag his back to his shack by the small lake.

Marty groaned in pain as he was dragged heartlessly across the ground. Taken into the killers shack he passed out from the pain after he bid the night goodbye. He didn't see a ghost but the killer was like a ghost, pretending to be a phantom as he kills curious college students and people that come to the forest. He was unaware that as Marty was dragged over the ground the contents of his pockets fell out. The shack wasn't much any more. The wood seemed damaged with holes but it held all sorts of weapons, and a chainsaw. Nobody could hear victims scream and they could be buried around there, but the killer was too lazy. Marty breathed his last breath as the killer finished him off. The fake phantom grabbed his chainsaw to help hide the body he had.

As the killer walked through the woods wishing he could find someone else, he found something from the contents of Marty's pocket;

a wallet. He opened it and found everything, his address, name, and ten dollars. It contained his driver's license and college ID. On a piece of paper was written his dorm address and room number along with his name. Someone in the office had written it down for him before school first started. Looking around for more, he saw something plastic and black, Marty's cell phone. Maybe Marty had friends. It was something for the killer to check out.

VIOLET AND BERNADETTE investigate

Marty's key in hand, they were driving off to Bernadette's dorm. "I know where Marty stayed. It had yellow tape on it. Let's go there. It's ok, no one will know and later we'll give the cops the key," Bernadette said.

Violet nodded knowing her mother wouldn't like that. "After the dorm let's go to the apartment. I'm not moving in yet."

"Why?" Bernie asked.

"The killer's around here. He knows he killed college students. He might be lurking," Violet answered.

"It's safer staying at the apartments ten minutes away, but that's ok. What if they don't catch him?" she asked driving.

"I don't know. I guess I'll have to move in anyways. My house is haunted," Violet said.

"Then let's help them catch this guy. Don't worry. We're here, and oh yea, we will definitely stop by the apartment. I've moved in it, just yesterday." The dorm was quiet. Not very many lights were on.

Marty's room was on the second floor. They went to a door with a keep out sign on it. Bernie tried the key. "Let's hope this works." She turned it and the knob opened the door. It was a mess. "I wonder if the killer broke in." She shut the front door. "Is anyone here?" she asked.

They looked around and found no one, and no sign of a struggle. They went to his room and sat down on the bed.

"I don't see anything strange. What do we do with the key?" Violet asked.

"I'll just go to the school office and tell them I found a key in the dorms parking lot. They may not ask any questions." Bernadette answered.

"I'm going to go to the bathroom." Violet went to the bathroom and turned on the sink water. "Water's on," she said and shut the door. After a minute she heard a squeak and thud out in the living room. Bernadette cried. The killer was there. He had killed four and now he wanted more. Violet opened the bathroom window and ran. It was quiet and she ran for the road. It might take a while but she could walk home. She needed to call the cops.

Suddenly, in the dark, a black clothed arm strong as an ox, grabbed her and started dragging her. After being tossed into a van she was tied up. "How did you k," she started to say wondering how he knew she had ran. She had jumped from a second story and landed on her feet hard. It was hard to walk fast at first.

His stone gray eyes stared. "Those windows are loud. I heard something. When I got to the bathroom, the window was wide open."

"Is Bernadette ok?" Violet asked.

"No, I cut her leg and knocked her over!" He was acting irritated by the question and hit her over the head so she would lay down. He closed the door, got in the van, and drove off.

Violet laid there miserable wondering what Bernadette was doing. Maybe she saved her from getting murdered, but it was obvious he was kidnapping her. He drove towards the highway and after a while it seemed he was probably headed for the haunted forest. She noticed he had taken off the mask so he didn't look so suspicious to the other drivers on the road. He could get caught that way, and if they stopped him and found her tied up that would look even worse. The stars twinkled as they approached country trees speeding along.

Abruptly he turned off the highway then into a wooded area. He parked in some trees. He was attempting to hide his parking though it did have and odd car crash look to it without the crash. He opened the door and tossed her over his shoulder. They didn't walk far before getting to a cave. He went in and put her down. He check her hands and feet to make sure they were completely tightly bound and walked away.

She hadn't seen any weapons so knew he wasn't ready to kill her, and by now Bernadette had called for help. She had her cell and the dorm also had a phone. The attack was reported and hopefully he was headed for Canada and couldn't hurt them. She twisted and scooted towards the cave opening. She could see him getting into the van and driving away. Her parents would soon be notified and she wanted them to know before twenty four hours. Violet would get very hungry by then.

She could hear the sounds of the night and got a little tired. As the crickets chirped it cooled off. Home was too far away to walk if she got free. It was obvious Violet would be spending the night at least. It was peaceful. An owl could be heard in the distance and the waxing moon provided light. She was lying against the small cave opening watching. "Hello," she called twice to see if any ghosts answered. During the night there were many strange sounds, but it was a forest. Violet didn't know what they were and she layed down in the dirt and leaves and closed her eyes.

Back at home Bonnie Tyler and her husband had received a very disturbing call, that her daughter's friend had been attacked at the dorm and Violet was missing. It would take almost an hour to walk home from the dorm and Violet hadn't showed up. Bernadette didn't know what happened to her. All she knew was she must have ran. "What was she doing taking my daughter to that dorm?" Bonnie asked her husband. He had no clue, but everyone stayed up half the night waiting to hear from Violet. The next day would start the biggest search. Bernadette had gotten away with only a small cut on her ankle.

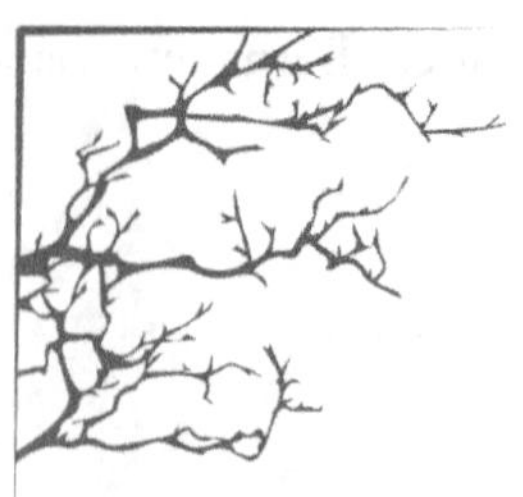

Chapter 10

The Wild

WAKING TO THE SOUND of birds, Violet hoped he would not come back to feed her. She wanted to eat berries and drink lake water but it wasn't safe. First she needed to get free of her ropes to walk properly. No one was there to save her and she was getting dirty. After sleeping, the ropes on her wrists and ankles was loose and she wiggled and twisted out of them. She crawled out of the cave and almost ran to the lakeside. Kneeling down in the damp dirt she took a drink out of clear looking water, then she spotted it. An abandoned row boat. It may not have been the killers. She went to it, sat down, then pushed off into the water. She needed to get out of there before he came back. She rowed out of sight in the middle of the large lake then stopped, drifting off in a large body of water.

The sun was shinning and a few birds sang. It wasn't too hot this September morning. Violet was hopeful. Soon she heard voices and sat up. She was coming to a camp. When the voices left she went to their sight and into their cooler taking a sandwich and soda. Hurrying quickly it was off to the boat and away from there. Paddling there was no sign of the road. It must have been a little bit off another way. It started to seem like sticking to the road would have been a better idea, but the killer could be on it. It was time to just eat her lunch. The only thing she had was her wallet with money in it. That could definitely come in handy, but first she needed to find civilization and get help. Her mother had to have been worried.

THE COPS HAD STOPPED by the Tyler house again. "We are going to look for her right now."

"What did Bernadette say?" Bonnie asked.

"She said only she was going to stay with her mother for a while now and your daughter that night wanted to go to their apartment. We searched the apartment and found nothing. We'll be all over this area and with dogs. And ma'am, we think there may be a chance he has taken her to the haunted forest, but if he has and he is the killer at large, he may kill her. We will send a helicopter to fly over it.

"What could we do?" Bonnie asked.

"Stay by the phone. Watch and listen for her. Let us know if you hear anything. I'll leave the police station number with you," the officer wrote down the number. "Fellas, let's go search the haunted forest." He waved goodbye and he and three other men were off to the forest. They were going first, then soon a search team would follow with dogs and in a few hours the helicopter would fly over. They could find Violet if she stayed there. What Bonnie heard made her afraid and she didn't want to leave her phone.

The dogs led the officers down the path and off to the old wooden shed. It smelled of rotten wood and old dried blood. When they pushed open the door it was a sight. Blood everywhere. They hoped it wasn't Violet's but they didn't think it was because it was so old. It became a crime scene and was blocked off. The helicopter flew over, but nobody found anything. Just Violet's boat. She had driven it to the right side of the lake. When the sheriff found out he decided to look that way.

They took the dogs to the boat. They had sniffed Violet's stuffed animals to know her scent and they jumped on the boat and barked indicating it was hers. That was the last area to search before late night fall.

Fifteen minutes down the road Violet had made it to a diner. Immediately she cleaned up in the bathroom then asked to use a phone. She called her mother glad to talk to her and tell her where she was. In a diner an hour away. "I'm not sure if I'm safe."

"Call the police Vi," her mother ordered.

Violet did as instructed and they weren't that far away. Tummy grumbling she ordered a small meal and sat away from the window. There were a lot of people in the diner that night. She looked as though she slept in the dirt, but she had combed her hair with her hands and washed herself in the sink. Now to get some food in her body and some energy. The waitress brought her a cheeseburger, fries, and drink. It looked so good. She poured the ketchup and went for it. "Are you going to be ok, honey?" the blond waitress asked concerned.

"Honestly, maybe. I called my mom. I'm a little far from home. My best friend is staying with her mom because the haunted forest slasher cut her ankle." She looked out the window. It was hard to see, but there he was. Her kidnapper, the devil she spoke of. He was watching her by a tree. "I called the police. I was there when my friend got attacked. I was kidnapped and got away, so I came here. I'm waiting for the cops. My kidnapper is right there." He saw them look and ran. "I can't leave. Please help me. I'm only eighteen."

"I'll go tell the manager. We'll keep an eye on you. I'll ask him what to do," the waitress responded and walked away with her blue dress twirling and her short blond hair cemented unable to move. Her name tag read Andrea.

As Violet ate she kept glancing out the window. The waitress came back. "We've called the cops. She said they were already on their way." Nobody was outside.

"Hopefully they will get here soon. Are you locking the door?" Violet asked.

"No, only if he looks threatening. Do you see his car?" Andrea asked.

"No, it looked like he was on foot." That moment four cop cars with their blue and red lights on came and stopped in the parking lot. They came in the diner and she stood up.

"Violet?" They asked. She nodded and went to them. "Get your stuff to go. They arrested the black forest killer. He's in that car there." The officer pointed to one. He waved to them and they left. Violet did not bother to point out he said the name of the forest wrong. "We spotted him sneaking around outside on our way here. He hasn't said anything. Was that him?" The officer asked already convinced it was.

She nodded. "Yes."

"I believe you. We have to make sure he is guilty of killing the three other people found in that forest."

"I don't think that forest is haunted. He tied me up and left me there over night in a cave. I slept and while I did the ropes became loose and I got away. But I never saw a single ghost." They started walking out the door. "I heard a lot of strange noises. Never knew what they were. Where's Bernadette? Is she ok?"

"Yes, she's at her mom's. Are you angry with her?" he asked.

"No, I was. I wanted to go to Marty's dorm room at first then I didn't. She also made me keep the key, and after that unexplained things happened in my house. I hope Marty's murder is solved." She got into the passenger's seat.

"What happened to that key?" He asked starting the car.

"We were attacked in his dorm. Either Bernadette has it or we left it in the door. It will be safe now I just don't know if I will live in the apartment now. She's the one going to that school, not me. Do I have to go to the police station?"

"No, I'll take you home."

AS VIOLET SAT ON HER couch with her blanket still dirty, an old furry friend landed on it and meowed. It was Inky. He even had his old collar! "When you went missing we called your aunt and she brought the cat so he could be a comforting surprise," her mother Bonnie said.

"I've decided not to move in with Bernie, at least for a while. As for now, I really need a shower." Violet dropped her cat and got up.

After her shower Violet put on her night shirt and plopped into bed, Inky right behind her. As the house got quiet and her parents went to bed she relaxed and used her cat as a pillow. As he purred there was a sound coming from the bathroom. When she went in she saw the ghost had written, Thank you in the steam. The ghost wouldn't be much of a problem any more. He had also signed it with an M so she knew it was Marty. A smiley face had been drawn in the corner of the mirror.

IN THE MORNING HER mom came in with pancakes and put them next her bed. "That killer had confessed last night to killing the three. They must have threatened him. His name was Mitchell something and he liked the haunted forest. He knew it pretty well. So don't worry any more. They will lock him up for good. Are you going to talk to Bernie?"

"I don't want to. I'll bet you she'll call." Violet checked her messages. There already was one from Bernadette. "In the message all she had to say was, 'Tell me all about it. Seemed a little insensitive to me. I guess I'll call her back. I don't know what to tell her about the apartment though. Oh well. I'll bet she doesn't want to live there either, or maybe. It's her school. Thanks mom." She held up the pancakes. "My favorite breakfast."

"No problem. What now?" her mom asked at the doorway.

"I go on. Go back to work. Divorce my husband."

"There's so much more to life than that," her mom said and left the room.

"I have yet to figure out what it is, what I was meant for. I am Violet Tyler. No one can take me down, Inky."

The cat jumped off the bed and went to her in agreement.

Don't miss out!

Visit the website below and you can sign up to receive emails whenever Martha Wickham publishes a new book. There's no charge and no obligation.

https://books2read.com/r/B-A-WPMHB-IRTBD

Connecting independent readers to independent writers.

About the Author

Martha Wickham is an author from OR. She has written 12 books since 2004.

Find more at www.marthawickham.com